You're invited to a . . .

Creepover

PJ Night

THE SHOW MUST GO ON!

First published in the United States in 2011 by Simon Spotlight,
an imprint of Simon & Schuster
First published in Great Britain in 2012 by Atom

Copyright © 2011 by Simon & Schuster, Inc.

Text by Michael Teitelbaum

YOU'RE INVITED TO A CREEPOVER is a trademark of Simon & Schuster, Inc.

A CIP catalogue record for this book
is available from the British Library.

ISBN 978-1-907411-26-7

Typeset in Manticore by M Rules
Printed and bound in Great Britain by
Clays Ltd, St Ives plc

Papers used by Atom are from well-managed forests
and other responsible sources.

PROLOGUE
THIRTY YEARS AGO …

"You're fired, Ms Wormhouse!" barked the head teacher of Moorwood Secondary School. "And we are cancelling your play, for ever." He leaned forward on his desk and locked his piercing gaze on the eyes of the woman seated across from him.

Mildred P. Wormhouse stared back, her dark, sunken eyes blazing with anger. "Cancelling?" she sneered. "I've worked on this play my entire life. Fire me if you wish, but the play will be performed!" Her curly shock of jet-black hair shook with every word.

"Maybe somewhere else," the head teacher said, standing now, his tone growing increasingly impatient. "But it will *not* be performed here, at this school – ever! Do you have such little regard for human life?"

"Bah!" Wormhouse snarled with a dismissive gesture. She stood, her long black coat flapping near her ankles as she turned away from the head teacher.

"A girl died last night, Ms Wormhouse," the head teacher said through clenched teeth. "On this school's stage, playing the lead in the play you wrote and directed. And that was only the final terrible incident. The rehearsals have been marred with accidents and other troubles. In fact, strange things have been happening at this school since the day you arrived. I've heard rumours that your play is cursed. I'm not a superstitious man, but I'm starting to believe them. I've seen to it that every last copy of the play has been thrown out."

Wormhouse turned slowly back towards the head teacher. "Cursed?" she hissed, her lips curling in a slight smile. "You really shouldn't let your fears get the best of you—"

"This conversation is over," the head teacher interrupted. He marched across the room and threw the door open. A roar erupted from the angry mob of parents and teachers who had gathered outside the office.

"There she is!" one man shouted.

"It's her fault," a woman yelled. "Her play!"

Wormhouse squirmed out of the door and through the crowd; her head bent low, her black coat flapping with every step like a cape. She headed for a corridor that led to the front door of the school. Pausing, she spun around to face the irate crowd.

"You may fire me," Wormhouse cried. "But you cannot stop my play. The show must go on." Then she turned down the corridor towards the front door of the building.

"Good riddance!" someone in the mob shouted.

"Don't ever show your face around here again!" screamed someone else.

Wormhouse disappeared from view around a corner in the corridor. But instead of turning left towards the front door, she headed right – towards the school's assembly hall, where her play had opened last night and where the girl playing the lead had died.

Walking quickly down the centre aisle of the empty assembly hall, glancing back over her shoulder every few steps, Wormhouse made her way backstage. Spotting an old steamer trunk, she shoved a pile of costumes off the top, then yanked open the lid. Inside the trunk were props from all the years of school productions. She reached into an inner pocket of her long coat and pulled out the last remaining copy of her play. Burying it beneath the mound of props inside the trunk, she gently lowered the lid.

Seething, her breath now laboured, she repeated her vow, muttering to herself, "The show must go on."

CHAPTER 1

Felix Gomez shoved aside a rack of hanging costumes and looked around backstage in the assembly hall of Moorwood Secondary School. He had been the Drama teacher at the school for a few years now, and he really wanted to do something different this year. He would put on a new play, he decided, not just the same old, same old. Tasked with revitalising the school's sagging theatre programme, he had spent weeks reading new plays, but so far nothing had grabbed him.

Then it started – an inexplicable urge, at first vague, then specifically focused on the backstage area of the school's assembly hall. Gomez had no idea why he was drawn back there, but somehow he knew that the obsessed, panicky state of mind that had gripped him for days now could only be eased by searching there.

In a dark corner, buried under long-discarded props and scenery, Gomez spotted an old steamer trunk. He knew instantly that this was what had been calling out to him, driving his obsession.

Throwing open the trunk, his hand – feeling as if it were being controlled by some other force – reached in. He pushed aside old props and grasped a stack of pages, bound together by three rusted metal fasteners.

Blowing off a cloud of dust from the top, Gomez read the title of the play: *The Last Sleepover*. He slammed the lid of the trunk and sat down in the dim light to read the play. It looked like it had been typed on a typewriter. "This is it!" he said to himself before he had read a single word. "I know it. This is the play I have been looking for!"

But as Gomez read the play, the force that had driven him here battled with a new feeling, one of inexplicable anxiety and horror. The more he read, the more intense the feeling of dread grew. Somewhere deep inside, he knew there was something wrong with the play.

"No. This isn't right," he muttered to himself, staring at the script, fighting the urge that had been driving him. "I can't do it. I won't put on this play."

Gomez stood and hurried to the trunk to put the play back where he'd found it. Feeling a sudden sharp pain in his ankle, he tripped over a low stool that he was certain had not been there a moment before. He crashed to the ground and clutched his right leg in pain.

Bree Hart paced up and down the centre aisle of the Moorwood Secondary School assembly hall and nervously twirled her curly dark hair around her finger. The meeting for pupils interested in auditioning for this year's play was about to begin. The assembly hall was filled with energised kids, busily chatting, eager to know what the play would be about. Bree had never felt this way before. She was partly excited and partly terrified.

"Trying to wear a hole through the carpet?" asked someone from behind Bree.

She spun around to face her best friend, Melissa Hwang.

"Oh, Lis, I'm so glad you came," Bree said, hugging her friend. "I'm so nervous!"

"I told you I would come," Melissa replied. "You think you're the only one who wants to be in the play?"

"I can't believe the time is here!" Bree exclaimed. "I've dreamed about acting for as long as I can remember, but I've never had the guts to actually audition for anything."

"Good for you, Bree," Melissa said. "You don't want to spend the rest of your life living in Megan's shadow, do you?"

Bree thought about her older sister, Megan, who had played the lead in every school play since Year 4. Melissa was right. It was time for Bree to take centre stage.

"I wonder what's keeping Mr Gomez," Bree said. "He was supposed to be here, like, ten minutes ago."

"Anxious to begin your new life in the theatre?" Melissa quipped.

"Something like that, yeah."

Just then the assembly hall door swung open.

"And here he is," Melissa said.

But instead of Mr Gomez, a tall woman strode slowly down the centre aisle, carrying a large briefcase. As she passed, Bree noticed the dark circles around her eyes and her jet-black hair.

"Who's that?" Bree whispered to Melissa. Melissa shrugged.

The woman climbed the steps to the stage and walked out to the centre. Adjusting the single microphone that had been set up for the auditions, she spoke in a surprisingly pleasant and gentle voice.

"Ladies and gentlemen, if I may have your attention, please," the woman began. "My name is Ms Hollows. Unfortunately, Mr Gomez had an accident yesterday afternoon. He broke his leg and will not be able to direct the play. I will be your substitute Drama teacher for the next few weeks, and I will be directing this year's play."

A buzz went through the crowd. Mr Gomez was one of the most popular teachers at the school – many of the pupils sitting in the assembly hall that afternoon were there because of him. Bree could hear the sighs of disappointment throughout the room.

"I was really looking forward to working with Mr Gomez," she moaned.

"Me too," Melissa concurred.

Having given the pupils a moment to digest this unexpected bit of news, Ms Hollows continued. "The play I have selected for us to perform is called *The Last Sleepover*."

Ms Hollows opened her briefcase and pulled out a

thick stack of papers. "I have copies of the play for those interested in auditioning," she said, placing the pile onto a stool next to where she stood. "Please form a line and come up and take a copy. You are to read the play this weekend and decide which role you would like to audition for. Auditions will be held after school on Monday. I will see you then."

One by one the pupils walked onto the stage, each taking a copy of the play. Bree felt a thrill run through her when she turned and looked out into the sea of empty seats in the assembly hall. She pictured herself in the lead role, standing before a cheering crowd, taking her bows, curtain call after curtain call.

"Are you all right, Gabrielle?" someone asked, startling Bree back to reality.

"Oh, yes, sorry, Ms Hollows," Bree said sheepishly as she picked up a copy of the play and hurried off the stage. Only after she left the stage did Bree realise that she had never told Ms Hollows her name, especially not her real name. Everyone, except sometimes her mother, called Gabrielle Hart by her nickname, Bree. *How did she know?* Bree wondered.

"Weird," she said under her breath.

"What's weird?" Melissa asked, falling into step with Bree.

"Somehow Ms Hollows knows my name already," Bree replied. "And not just my nickname. My *real* name. No one ever guesses that Bree is short for Gabrielle."

"Well, you are one of the top pupils in the school," Melissa pointed out. "Maybe she did some research about who she might want in the play."

"Yeah, maybe," Bree replied, not really believing what Melissa had just said. "Anyway, I'll see you later, Lis."

Melissa waved as she ran towards her bus. "Bye."

Later that evening Bree curled up in a big, overstuffed chair in her living room and opened the script. *"The Last Sleepover,"* she read aloud, "by M. P. Wormhouse." Bree read on.

The play told the story of a house haunted by the ghost of a girl who had always wanted to attend a sleepover. As Bree got further and further into the script, she began to read aloud:

"(CARRIE'S BEDROOM IN HER NEW HOUSE. THE HOUSE IS AN OLD VICTORIAN ONE

THAT IS BEING REMODELLED AND HAS AN ABANDONED, HAUNTED FEEL TO IT. THE TWO OTHER GIRLS WHO HAVE GATHERED AT THE SLEEPOVER ARE HUDDLED AROUND CARRIE. CARRIE SITS IN THE MIDDLE, WITH HER BLACK CAT ON HER LAP.)

CARRIE: Thanks for coming tonight. Ready to hear something creepy?

RACHEL (EXCITED): Awesome!

LAURA (NERVOUS): What?

(CARRIE LEANS IN CLOSE TO THE GIRLS TO TELL THEM HER SECRET.)

CARRIE: Years ago, a girl named Millie lived in this house. She was a shy girl who kept to herself most of the time. Although she didn't have a lot of friends, the thing she wanted most in the world was to be invited to a sleepover. She dreamed about hanging out all night in her pyjamas, in a sleeping bag, telling stories, eating, laughing ...

RACHEL: Having pillow fights.

CARRIE: Having pillow fights. All the cool stuff we're doing tonight. Anyway, Millie waited and waited until finally a girl named Gabby had a sleepover. Gabby invited every girl in her class - every girl, that is, except Millie.

RACHEL: Mean!

LAURA: Poor Millie.

CARRIE: I know. Gabby was a bit of a bully. Millie begged her to be allowed to come to the sleepover, but every time she asked, Gabby said no.

RACHEL: Why?

CARRIE: I don't know, but that sleepover was only the first of many. At least twice a year, Gabby had a huge sleepover, and each time all the girls in the class were invited except Millie. Then Millie got sick. Very sick. In time she died, having never got her wish to attend a sleepover.

LAURA: That is so sad!

RACHEL: It is. But where does the creepy part come in?

CARRIE: I'm getting there. Millie's family moved shortly after her death and sold this house to another family. That family had a little girl. One night, that girl had a sleepover. And that's when the haunting began. Lights flickered on and off, and a strange face appeared outside her bedroom window.

RACHEL: Yeah, right. You're making this up.

CARRIE: I'm not. Promise. I heard the whole story from the old woman who lives next door. She remembers Millie. They went to school together a very long time ago.

LAURA: Creepy.

CARRIE: It gets creepier. Every girl who has had a sleepover in this house since Millie died has experienced the same things. It's said that Millie's ghost haunts this house and will keep haunting it until she is allowed into a sleepover!

RACHEL: Well, she's not getting into this one!

CARRIE: Nope. Not if I have anything to say about it.

(LIGHTS GO OUT ALL OF A SUDDEN. GIRLS SCREAM WITH FEAR.)"

As Bree continued to read the play, she began to get more and more creeped out.

"This play is so dark ... and there's something else I can't quite put my finger on," she murmured to herself when she had finished reading. She set the script aside. "I wish Ms Hollows was putting on a happy play, with singing or something. Maybe I should wait to audition next year." But that didn't make Bree feel any better either.

Bree recalled her English teacher describing the feeling of being outside your comfort zone. That the best way to learn and grow was to do something that felt difficult or unfamiliar. Maybe this was the play for her, and maybe she was destined to play Carrie.

"Whatcha got there?"

"Oh, hey, Megan," Bree said absentmindedly, not bothering to look up at her sister. "It's a copy of the play we're putting on this year."

"Are you seriously thinking of auditioning?" Megan asked, unable to stifle a giggle. "The shy, fly-on-the-wall, always-stays-in-background Bree wants to step into the spotlight?"

"You're always such a drama queen, Megan," Bree replied. "It's just a play. It's just an audition. Are you nervous that you aren't the only one in this family with acting talent?"

"OK, OK, don't get all riled up," Megan shot back. "I'm just teasing you. So, what's the play about?"

Bree described the strange story of *The Last Sleepover* to her sister.

"Sounds creepy," Megan said when Bree had finished recounting the plot.

"It really is," Bree said, hoping to get Megan's advice about acting. "Just reading it gives me a really weird feeling. Have you ever been in a play like this? You know, where it just gets under your skin?"

"That's nuts," Megan replied with a laugh. "It's just a play. It's just acting, you know, make-believe. I hate to break it to you, but there is no such thing as the bogeyman, or ghosts, or other silly stuff like that. You know what I think?"

"Enlighten me," Bree said.

"It's nerves," Megan said. "You might just not be cut out for the stage."

"Thanks for the sisterly advice!" Bree shouted as her sister left the room. Just when she thought Megan might be of help, she acted like, well, like Megan. "You know what I think? I think you just don't want to share the spotlight with me. Well, guess what? I *am* auditioning and I *will* get the lead!"

Bree picked up the script and stormed off to her room. She would show Megan!

But that night, as Bree drifted off to sleep, she had to

admit to herself that she did feel nervous. She couldn't shake the haunting presence of the play and its characters. They felt so real, as if they had entered her life, not as words on a written page but as real people, including a very real-seeming ghost.

She spent the night, tossing and turning, her dreams blending with her waking thoughts. It was the first of many restless nights.

CHAPTER 2

Bree was distracted during lessons all day on Monday. She could focus on one thing and one thing only – the audition. Each class seemed like it lasted for three hours. She couldn't wait for the school day to be over so she could finally get her big chance.

When the last bell rang, Bree raced to the assembly hall. She couldn't decide what she felt more: excited or nervous. She decided it was pretty much a tie. Reaching the assembly hall, she took a deep breath, opened the door, and walked in.

"Bree!" Melissa called out as soon as Bree had stepped into the assembly hall. She waved from the front, up near the edge of the stage. "Here!"

Bree hurried down the centre aisle to join her friend.

"What did you think of the script?" Melissa asked. "Wasn't it spooky?"

"It totally creeped me out," said Bree. "I wanted to put it down, but it was like something forced me to keep reading."

"I know, I know!" Melissa exclaimed. "That Wormhouse must have been some kind of writer. I had to keep going until I got to the end . . . like, *had* to keep reading, not just because I wanted to. And the whole time I kept thinking, 'I really want to be in the play . . . but *this* play?' But then I got such a strong urge to do it, I have to at least try out.

"I'm going to read for the part of Rachel, Carrie's best friend," Melissa continued. "I need to set my sights on something I think I can handle."

"I'm going for Carrie, Lis," Bree said. "It's time for me to jump into the deep end."

"How cool would it be if we got to play best friends in the play?" Melissa squealed with excitement.

"Yeah, well, that's not going to happen," said someone right beside them. Bree didn't even have to turn her head to know who had spoken. It was Tiffany O'Brian, one of the most popular – and snobbiest – girls in the school.

"Really?" Melissa replied. "And why is that?"

"Because *I'm* getting the lead," Tiffany replied. "This audition is a waste of time. I'll be playing Carrie. This reading is merely a formality."

Bree never ceased to be amazed by the size of Tiffany's ego and her boundless sense of entitlement.

"Just because you've played the lead before doesn't mean you'll be the lead in this one," Bree pointed out.

"Well, look who's speaking up," Tiffany taunted. "Little Miss Wallflower, never dances at a party, never says two words. And you are suddenly going to get the lead. I think if anything you're more suited to play the ghost."

"Leave her alone, Tiffany," Melissa chimed in. "She's allowed to audition just like you are."

"Waste your time if you like, Wallflower," Tiffany said, tossing back her wavy blond hair. "But the part is mine." Then she turned and walked to the other side of the assembly hall.

"She's the worst," Melissa said when Tiffany had gone.

"Must be nice being Miss Perfect," Bree added. "I wonder how it feels. Maybe I should ask my sister."

The door to the assembly hall swung open, and Ms Hollows walked down the aisle and up onto the stage.

"Ladies and gentlemen, did we all enjoy the script?"

she asked, scanning the assembly hall from one side to the other.

Murmurs, grunts and nods of agreement passed through the assembled pupils.

"Very well then," she said. "Let's begin. Will those auditioning for the role of Carrie please line up to my left, here on the stage?"

This is it, Bree thought. *No turning back now.* She joined four other girls up on the stage. Tiffany, seeming to be in no hurry, was last in line. *She probably thinks she'll watch the rest of us, then go last and blow us all away,* Bree thought as she watched the first girl walk over to Ms Hollows in the centre of the stage. *And who knows? Maybe she's right.*

Bree glanced at the girl performing a scene, but she really didn't hear any of the lines. Her focus was locked on the script and the lines she was going to read.

"Next," Ms Hollows called when the first girl had finished. Bree swallowed hard and walked briskly to the centre of the stage.

"And which scene have you chosen, Gabrielle?" Ms Hollows asked. This time Bree was less startled when the Drama teacher used her full name. She decided Melissa must have been onto something yesterday. *She must have looked me up in the school records,* she thought.

"I'm going to do Carrie's monologue during the 'floating objects' scene," Bree answered.

"Very well. Begin."

Bree had thought about who Carrie was. She wanted to become another person, not just be herself reading the lines. Megan was wrong. Acting was more than just pretending. She was going to *become* Carrie. Bree began:

```
I told you. This house is haunted by
the girl who died before she ever got
invited to a sleepover. Her name was
Millie, and now she shows up every
time someone has a sleepover in this
house. I feel sort of sorry for her,
but she is a ghost. And who wants a
ghost at their sleepover? I know, I
know, it sounds nuts that I'm
standing here talking about a ghost
like she's just some girl who lives in
the neighbourhood, but somehow I
think she's really connected to this
house. Well, it's my house now, not
hers, and she's just not invited. End
of story. I know you don't believe me
about Millie, but don't be surprised
if--
```

Instinctively, Bree paused onstage, as the stage directions called for the girls at the sleepover to laugh and throw pillows at Carrie. Then a hairbrush and a small handheld mirror on the dressing table float up into the air. The brush moves in long, even strokes. The mirror remains stationary. Suddenly a face appears in the mirror – and only in the mirror – the face of a young girl brushing her long jet-black hair. All the characters scream, except for Carrie.

After the brief pause, Bree continued with the lines:

```
I told you! I told you the ghost is
real. Millie, is that you? If so, you
are not welcome! This sleepover is for
the living only!
```

This was the moment Bree was waiting for in the audition. She was to pretend to be horrified as the brush stops moving and both the brush and mirror drop to the ground, the glass in the mirror shattering all over the stage. Then Bree let out her best horror-movie scream.

"Thank you, Gabrielle," Ms Hollows said when the scene was over. "Next!"

Bree left the stage and took a seat in the front row. She could feel the adrenaline that had fuelled her audition still coursing through her.

She then watched as two other girls auditioned for the

role of Carrie. Although Tiffany did a good job, Bree was confident it was no better than the audition she had given. She suddenly felt sure of herself, thinking that she could really do this, that she was as good as anyone up there.

Auditions for the role of Rachel were next. Three girls auditioned, including Melissa. When Melissa had finished, she rushed over and sat next to Bree.

"You were great!" Bree said.

"So were you!" Melissa echoed. "That was an amazing scream. You were way better than Tiffany any old day."

One by one, Ms Hollows called out the rest of the roles, and groups of pupils went up and read. When everyone had auditioned, Ms Hollows spoke into the microphone.

"Thank you all," she said. "The cast list will be posted tomorrow." As Bree and Melissa got up to leave, Ms Hollows brushed past them. She turned back, looked Bree right in the eye, and whispered, "The play has been waiting for you." Then she hurried from the assembly hall.

"What was that?" Melissa asked, seeing that her friend was obviously shaken.

"I – I don't know," Bree murmured. "Does that mean I got the lead?"

CHAPTER 3

Bree lay awake in bed, staring at the ceiling. She turned her head and glanced at her alarm clock. It read two-thirty.

Will I ever fall asleep? she wondered. She couldn't get Ms Hollow's words out of her mind. *The play has been waiting for you.* What in the world did that mean?

She recalled the eerie feeling she'd had when she first read the play. As much as she wanted to put it down, another part of her felt drawn to the play. She felt as if she had to audition, and now she might actually be getting the lead. *Is that what Ms Hollows meant?*

Bree looked over at the clock again. Two-thirty-five. Rolling over onto her side so she couldn't see the clock, she forced her eyes closed. Much to her surprise, she dozed off.

When the alarm went off at six-thirty the next

morning, Bree woke with a start. She was confused for a moment about where she was exactly. She knew she had been dreaming – deep, intense dreams – but she couldn't remember anything about them. Realising that she was still safe in her own bed, she threw off the covers and started to get ready for school.

"Today's the day," she murmured to herself as she slipped on her dressing gown. She didn't totally expect to get the lead, but just for fun, she imagined what it would be like to take her bow on opening night. She was stretching her arms way out and bending over when she accidentally knocked into the small handheld mirror sitting on her dressing table. It shattered on the floor.

"Gabrielle, is everything OK?" her mum shouted from downstairs.

"Yes, everything's fine!" Bree replied.

Just seven years of bad luck, that's all, she thought as she quickly swept up the shattered pieces. She then headed downstairs for breakfast, her delusions of grandeur trailing behind her.

As she entered the school building a short while later, Bree glanced quickly at the time on her mobile phone. She still had a few minutes before registration, so she dashed to the assembly hall. Stepping up to the noticeboard outside the door, she took a deep breath and scanned the board. Nothing! No cast list yet. She'd have to wait.

Struggling to pay attention in her first lesson, Bree bolted from her seat when the bell rang. Navigating the corridors, cutting and skipping around people like a winger on a football field, she hurried to the assembly hall. There she found a crowd of pupils gathered in front of the noticeboard.

Before she could reach the board, Bree spotted Melissa, who shrieked, "You got it! You got it!"

Bree squirmed through the crowd and shoved her face up to the board. There, hanging by a drawing pin, was the cast list. Next to the name "Carrie" it said "Gabrielle Hart".

Bree was stunned. Her wish had come true! She had got the lead!

"And I got Rachel!" Melissa added, pointing to her own name on the list, right below Bree's.

"I – I can't believe this," Bree said, for a moment not knowing whether to celebrate or to run and hide.

"If you think *you* can't believe it, wait until Tiffany finds out!" Melissa said.

"Wait until I find out what?"

Tiffany shoved her way to the front of the crowd. Her eyes opened wide and she pursed her lips together tightly as she read down the list. "Ugh. This is so wrong!" she whined.

"What's wrong about it, Tiffany?" Melissa asked. "You auditioned; Bree auditioned. She got the part."

"But I am so much better than her," Tiffany complained. "I have to be in this play."

"But you are in the play," Melissa pointed out. "You've been cast as Millie, the ghost who haunts Carrie's sleepover. It looks like *you're* more suited to play the ghost." She caught Bree's eye and winked, holding back a giggle at her own joke.

"It'll be fun to work together, Tiffany," Bree said. In a weird way she felt sorry for Tiffany. It meant so much to her to play the lead.

"I don't need your pity, Wallflower," Tiffany barked. Then she turned and stalked away from the crowd.

"See you at rehearsal, Tif!" Melissa called after her.

"Lis, don't," Bree said. "The more upset you make her, the more she's going to take it out on me."

"Oh please, Bree," Melissa said as the crowd began to break up and head off to their lessons. "She's got to grow up. She can't always get everything she wants. You won that role fair and square."

"I wonder," Bree replied, her thoughts drifting back to the previous day. *The play has been waiting for you.*

"What do you mean?" Melissa asked.

"What? Oh, nothing. I've got to get to my next lesson. I'll see you at rehearsal."

"See you at rehearsal . . . *Carrie!*" Melissa called out.

"Goodbye, *Rachel!*" Bree shouted back. She was thrilled that her best friend would be there with her every step of the way. But there would still be Tiffany to deal with, not to mention the play itself.

At the first rehearsal that afternoon, Bree made her way to the assembly hall. Stepping inside, she found a group of pupils up on the stage, hard at work putting together the set for the show.

Many plays had been performed in this assembly hall over the four decades since the secondary school had opened. And so it was no problem for the kids who had volunteered to work behind the scenes on the play to rummage through old scenery and props to make a new set.

The main set for the play was Carrie's bedroom. Bree stared at the stage, watching the set decorators hard at work. They had been at it for only a little while, but she could see that when it was completed, it really would look as if Carrie lived in a haunted house. The walls of Carrie's bedroom, which now stood stacked in a row waiting to be set up, were cracked and peeling. Cobwebs dangled from the corners.

A dusty, damaged chandelier sat on the stage, waiting to be hung. When it was fully wired, it would flicker on and off as, offstage, a pupil operated a light switch set up to control the chandelier.

A spotlight was being set up. It would be placed outside a fake window built into one of the walls. Turning this spotlight on and off quickly would create the illusion of lightning flashing outside during a thunderstorm scene.

On the back side of the window, a pair of tattered old shutters hung loosely. Poles attached to the bottom of these shutters would allow unseen pupils backstage to flap them during the storm scene, as if the wind were fiercely blowing them back and forth against the house. An old piece of tin with a handle on the bottom hung backstage. When a pupil shook the tin sheet, it sounded like thunder.

Bree smiled widely, picturing all these elements coming together on the finished set to create Carrie's bedroom – *her* bedroom.

"Boo!"

Bree jumped, startled by Melissa's sudden entrance.

"Don't sneak up on a person in a haunted house," Bree scolded her best friend. "Even if it's not finished yet. Don't you know anything?"

"I know that Tiffany is still sulking," Melissa replied.

Bree turned to face the back of the room and saw Tiffany sitting by herself, flipping through her copy of the play, shaking her head in disapproval.

Ms Hollows entered the assembly hall and hurried down the centre aisle. She paused at the foot of the stage for a moment, taking in the vista of Carrie's bedroom. Then, giving a quick nod of approval, she climbed the stairs and walked out to centre stage.

"Ladies and gentlemen," she began. The buzz of excited conversation that had been humming through the assembly hall stopped instantly. "I thank you all again for volunteering to be a part of this play. Thank you to the set decorators and technical volunteers. Now, may I have all the actors up onstage, please?"

"Here we go, Bree!" Melissa said excitedly as the two made their way onto the stage with the rest of the actors, including Tiffany, playing the ghost; the boy playing Carrie's elderly neighbour; and the boy and girl playing Carrie's parents, as well as a few others.

"Yeah, here we go," Bree echoed, still unable to shake the twin feelings of excitement and nervousness.

"Ready to put on a fantastic play, everyone?" Ms Hollows addressed the cast. The actors on stage nodded, some more vigorously than others. Bree was somewhere in the middle. Tiffany's eyes were glued to the floor.

"All right then," Ms Hollows continued. "Let's start from the top. Scene one. Rachel, Laura and Carrie. Places, please."

Bree, Melissa and Dara Marinelli, the girl who'd been chosen to play Laura, sat in a circle in the middle of the stage. They began rehearsing the scene.

RACHEL: Nice, Carrie. The place looks like it was decorated by a wrecking ball!

CARRIE: Cute. You know we only moved in a few weeks ago. My family and I haven't had a chance to do it up yet. I just couldn't wait to have my first sleepover. It helps to make it feel like home.

LAURA: Yeah, if your home's been condemned!

CARRIE: Ha-ha-ha! Come on, you guys. We should--

(SUDDENLY LIGHTNING FLASHES AND THUNDER RUMBLES.)

LAURA: Eiii!

CARRIE: Laura?

LAURA: Sorry, I'm just a little afraid of thunder. I--

(THE THUNDER SOUNDS AGAIN ... LOUDER THIS TIME. LAURA SCOOTS OVER CLOSER TO CARRIE. SUDDENLY THE CHANDELIER OVERHEAD FLICKERS ON AND OFF, AGAIN AND AGAIN.)

RACHEL: OK, now I'm officially creeped out. I--

CARRIE: Look!

(CARRIE POINTS TO THE CHANDELIER. A FLASH OF LIGHTNING REVEALS THAT THE CHANDELIER IS SHAKING UNCONTROLLABLY. EVERYONE SCREAMS.)

"OK, let's take a break, everyone," Ms Hollows called out. "Very good start."

As the girls in the cast sat down on the edge of the stage to get their notes from Ms Hollows, the lights in the assembly hall began to flicker again. But this time it was not just the stage lights that flashed on and off. Every light in the room twinkled.

"Please leave the lights on!" Ms Hollows shouted impatiently to the technical crew backstage.

"It's not us, Ms Hollows!" Tyler Lahari, the boy running the lights, replied, sticking his head out from backstage. "We didn't touch the lights that time!"

Then the entire assembly hall went completely dark.

CHAPTER 4

"Torches!" Ms Hollows shouted out.

Several members of the backstage crew came running out with their torches blazing.

"I'm going to see if I can find out what's going on with the lights. Perhaps the whole school has lost power," Ms Hollows said, and left the assembly hall.

"Great, now what do we do?" asked Bree.

"I have an idea," Melissa said. "Why don't we sit in a circle and pretend this is a real sleepover?"

"We could even tell ghost stories to get us in the mood," Tiffany added. "Unless, of course, you can't handle it, Wallflower."

"I'm fine," Bree said. "I guess it can only help us get more deeply into our characters."

As the backstage crew settled into the front row of the assembly hall, the girls onstage flipped on their torches and sat on their pillows.

"I'll go first," Melissa said. "Here's one I heard last summer.

"A girl went to a school disco. She was quite shy and was sitting in a corner when a nice-looking boy came over and asked her if she wanted to dance. No one else had even come near her, so she jumped at the chance.

"The girl was surprised that she had never seen the boy at school before. He told her that he used to go to the school a few years earlier but had moved away and that he always tried to come back for the school dances, since he liked them so much and they always brought back so many good memories for him.

"The two danced every dance, and soon it was time to leave. The boy offered to walk the girl home, saying that her house was on the way to his house anyway. During the walk, the girl got cold, and the boy offered her his school jacket, which had his name stitched onto the front. He draped it over her shoulders, and she felt warmer right away.

"When they reached the girl's house, the boy kissed

her good night and went on his way. Once inside the door, the girl realised that the boy's school jacket was still on her shoulders.

"She turned to shout to him, but he was nowhere to be seen. It had been only a minute since he'd left, but the street was now dark and empty.

"Then the girl remembered that while they were walking, the boy had mentioned where he lived. She hurried to his house, which was only about ten minutes away. When she arrived, the girl stepped up to the front door and rang the bell.

"A woman answered the door. The girl asked if the boy was home, guessing that he had to be. Where else would he have gone? The woman's eyes filled with tears as she explained that the boy was her son and that he had died three years earlier.

"'But that's impossible!' the girl exclaimed. 'I just saw him at the school dance. In fact, he lent me his jacket. Here it is!'

"The woman took the coat and hugged it tightly as tears flowed from her eyes. 'Thank you for returning this,' she said. 'My son died in an accident at a school dance three years ago. I wanted his school jacket as a memento, but the people at the school said they never found it. Thank you for bringing it home!'"

The girls onstage breathed out a collective sigh. Each girl, without even realising it, had slid off her pillow and was clutching it tightly.

"That was great," Bree said to Melissa.

"Pretty creepy," Dara added. "I heard one once that my cousin told when my family went up to my aunt and uncle's holiday house. We were sitting around a campfire, and my cousin told us the story of a school tour group on a trip to the Lake District.

"A small group of kids got separated from the main group and found themselves in front of an old house that looked like it hadn't been touched for centuries.

"'This is not on the tour,' one of the friends said. 'I don't think we should go in.'

"'Come on,' said another. 'The tour is boring. Maybe we'll find something cool in there.'

"The group slowly pushed open the creaky old front door and stepped inside. The door slammed shut behind them loudly, startling everyone in the group. Then a man dressed in full medieval costume stepped into the entryway.

"'Good day to you,' the man said. 'Welcome to my home. My name is Hadrian Cartwright.'

"'I thought you said that this house wasn't on the tour,' one friend whispered to another.

"'It's not supposed to be. I guess they added it or something.'

"As Hadrian Cartwright led the group on a tour of the house, he described the day-to-day activities of his daily life in medieval times. The friends were all impressed by his detailed descriptions.

"'This guy's the best actor yet,' one friend whispered.

"'Yeah, but you'd think they would clean the house up before they took people on a tour,' said another. 'This place is a filthy wreck.'

"Just as the tour ended, the kids heard the front door burst open.

"'Hey! Who's in here?' someone shouted.

"The kids ran towards the voice and found themselves face-to-face with a police officer. 'What are you kids doing in here?' he asked them as he stepped inside.

"'We were taking the tour,' one of the pupils explained.

"'The tour?' the officer replied. 'What tour? This house has been closed up and condemned for years.'

"'But what about Mr Cartwright, the tour guide?'

"'Cartwright? Hadrian Cartwright?' the officer asked.

"'Yeah, that's him.'

"'Hadrian Cartwright lived in this house seven hundred years ago! You say you saw him?'

"'Yeah, he's right over—'

"The kids all turned to the spot where a moment before, Hadrian Cartwright had been standing. He had vanished. Turning back to the police officer, their eyes opened wide in shock as they watched the front door slam closed . . . with no one having touched it.

"'Goodbye, Hadrian,' the officer said, which was when the kids realised that they had been given a tour of the house by its original occupant – or at least by his ghost."

"Cool!" Melissa cried. "I like it. But I wish the lights would come back on so we could keep rehearsing."

"I have one," Tiffany said with a sly grin. "My story is about the very play we're performing," Tiffany began. "I did a little research and discovered that it was first performed thirty years ago. In fact, it was put on in this school, in this assembly hall, on this stage where we are now sitting.

"A creepy Drama teacher named Wormhouse wrote the play. She insisted that the school put it on, but she met a lot of resistance from parents and teachers who said it was too strange and too scary and that it didn't have a happy ending. They all wanted Wormhouse to do a safe, nice musical, something everyone knew and was comfortable with. But she would have no part of that. She insisted that her play be performed, and in the end she got her way.

"Right from the start, though, the rehearsals were plagued with strange incidents. Props would break, scenery would collapse for no reason right in the middle of a scene, and lights would go on and off by themselves – kind of like what happened to us tonight.

"Finally opening night came. But as soon as the girl playing Carrie stepped out onto the stage to begin the show, something fell from above. It struck her and killed her instantly."

All the girls onstage gasped.

Tiffany had them in the palm of her hand, and she knew it.

"Back then there were rumours that the play itself is cursed . . . and that whoever plays the lead is destined to die!"

As Tiffany said the word "die", the lights in the assembly hall blazed back to life.

Bree looked around and realised that everyone on the stage was wide eyed – and they were all staring right at her!

CHAPTER 5

"Thank you, Tiffany, for that very entertaining piece of folklore," Ms Hollows said as she came back into the assembly hall. "As you can see, the problem with the lights has been resolved. Now if we can all get back to reality, I'd like to run through one more scene."

Bree did her best to focus as the rehearsal continued, but Tiffany's story had really shaken her. *Cursed!* she thought. *Could the play really be cursed?* Was that what she had been feeling all along? Was such a thing even possible?

Bree was by nature a pretty rational, straightforward person. She liked ghost stories but never truly believed in the supernatural. But a strange feeling of dread began to work its way into her subconscious. She was sure she wanted to be here doing this play. But there was something else ... something she just couldn't put her finger on that was making her question that decision.

When rehearsal ended, she headed from the assembly hall feeling unsatisfied. She thought that the first part of the rehearsal had gone very well. Then the lights had gone out and Tiffany had told her story. Bree was much less pleased with the quality of the scenes she had run through after that.

"You OK?" Melissa asked, catching up to Bree at the front door of the school. "You seemed a bit out of it during that last scene."

"I don't know, Lis, that story Tiffany told about the play really freaked me out," Bree explained.

"Oh, she's just trying to get under your skin," Melissa said. "She's still all bent out of shape about not getting the lead. She's probably trying to rattle you so Ms Hollows reconsiders. Don't let her mess with your mind. You're doing a great job. You were born to be Carrie!"

"Thanks, Lis. I think," Bree said hesitantly. She knew that Melissa's comment was intended as a compliment, but it reminded her of what Ms Hollows had said on the day of the auditions: *The play has been waiting for you.* Both statements carried a strange sense of destiny that made Bree very uncomfortable.

Bree and Melissa stepped out of the building and into a raging thunderstorm.

"OK, well, that explains why the lights went out," Bree said, looking out at the wind-whipped trees and sheets of torrential rain. She felt relieved to find a logical explanation for the creepy incident that had so closely mimicked the events in the play.

"Definitely," Melissa agreed. "I just hope I have power at home. I have tons of chatting to do online! See ya tomorrow, Bree." Melissa trotted over to where her older brother waited in his car to give her a lift home.

"Hi, *Gabrielle*," said someone from behind her. Bree spun around and saw Tiffany standing on the steps of the school.

"Tiffany!" Bree cried, startled to hear a classmate calling her by her full name.

"I have something to tell you," Tiffany said.

Bree thought she had said quite enough for one day already. Or was she actually going to apologise for always being so snotty?

"OK," Bree said cautiously.

"You're going to *hate* playing the lead," Tiffany spat out, contempt dripping from every word. "In fact, you're going to be sorry that you ever even tried out for this play."

"What do you mean?" she asked.

"The amount of work is intense," Tiffany continued, stepping up right next to Bree. "Learning all those lines. All the pressure of the whole play revolving around you. Everyone is depending on you, you know. That's what comes with being the lead. And it's so easy to let down the whole cast ... the whole school, actually. One little mistake, one tiny thing done wrong, and you could ruin the play for everyone."

Bree was startled and, for the moment, speechless.

"I'd quit now if I were you," Tiffany said as she brushed past Bree. Then she stopped and turned back towards her. "But fortunately, I'm not you."

Bree watched Tiffany disappear into the driving rain and darkness, stunned and confused. She got onto the late bus for pupils who were involved in after-school activities, her mind still reeling from the bizarre encounter with Tiffany.

Was that a threat?

After dinner, Bree hunkered down at her desk and dived into what felt like a week's worth of homework. As she ploughed through her Maths and Science questions, she wondered how Megan had managed to be in all those school plays, for all these years, while remaining a straight-A pupil.

"Have a good day, Superstar?" Megan asked, poking her head into Bree's room, startling her.

"Pretty good," Bree said. She was not about to share all that had happened with Tiffany that afternoon. Megan would probably say that Tiffany was right. *I'm not giving her any reason to put me down again. I'm sure she'd love to see me flop . . . or even better, quit.*

"Well, be sure to let me know if you need any acting tips," Megan offered.

"Yeah, right, Megan," Bree replied sarcastically. "You'll be the first one I'll go to."

Megan shrugged and closed the door.

After another hour of homework, Bree began to feel sleepy. She had got a good chunk done and felt satisfied. Slipping into bed, she read for about five minutes before drifting off to sleep.

In her dream, Bree found herself sitting in the front

row of the school's assembly hall. The props and scenery for *The Last Sleepover* were set up on the stage. "How did I get here?" she wondered aloud.

A crowd of people filed into the assembly hall and took their seats.

"What am I doing sitting in the audience?" Bree wondered. "I should be backstage, or up on the stage, or . . ."

At that moment she noticed that something was wrong. Glancing around at the people entering the assembly hall, she realised that they looked strange. *What are they all wearing? And what's with that hair? They all look like they stepped out of another era.*

Was it an eighties theme night at the school? But why would they do that on the night of a performance? And why would they ask the audience to dress up as well? None of it made any sense.

The lights went down and the actors made their way onto the stage in the dark. Dim stage lights set the mood, and the play began.

    RACHEL: Nice, Carrie. The place looks
    like it was decorated by a wrecking
    ball!

CARRIE: Cute. You know we only moved in a few weeks ago. My family and I haven't had a chance to do it up yet. I just couldn't wait to have my first sleepover. It helps to make it feel like home.

LAURA: Yeah, if your home's been condemned!

That's the scene we just rehearsed today, Bree thought. Then she focused on the girls up onstage. OK, now this is officially weird. Even the actors have hairstyles from another era.

As the play continued, Bree grew more and more confused.

(SUDDENLY LIGHTNING FLASHES AND THUNDER RUMBLES.)

LAURA: Eiii!

CARRIE: Laura?

LAURA: Sorry, I'm just a little afraid of thunder. I--

(THE THUNDER SOUNDS AGAIN ... LOUDER THIS TIME. LAURA SCOOTS OVER NEXT TO CARRIE. SUDDENLY THE CHANDELIER OVERHEAD FLICKERS ON AND OFF, AGAIN AND AGAIN.)

RACHEL: OK, now I'm officially creeped out. I--

CARRIE: Look!

(CARRIE POINTS TO THE CHANDELIER. A FLASH OF LIGHTNING REVEALS THAT THE CHANDELIER IS SHAKING.)

Bree heard a sharp snapping sound that seemed to be coming from overhead. Looking up, panic flooded through her as she realised that a stage light had broken loose and was plunging down from above. The light was headed right for the girl playing Carrie!

CHAPTER 6

"Look out!" Bree screamed, leaping from her seat.

The stage vanished, as did the girl and the falling light and the audience. Bree was sitting upright in her bed, her heart pounding and her hands shaking. After a few seconds, her mind cleared and she realised that she had just awakened from a terrible dream. She was in her room at home, and the sun was shining through her window.

It was like I was right there, when the play was first performed. And that poor girl getting hit by the light. Thank you, Tiffany, for planting that vision in my brain.

Trying to shake off the effects of the dream, Bree pulled herself together and headed downstairs for breakfast.

"You look horrible," Megan said when Bree joined her at the kitchen table.

"Thanks. I didn't sleep well. Bad dreams."

"About what?" Megan asked.

"The show," Bree replied through her sleepy haze. She immediately regretted having shared that with her sister.

"Stage fright, huh?" Megan said casually, shoving another spoonful of cereal into her mouth.

"No," Bree replied defensively. "I'm fine when I'm onstage. It's just the play itself. It's hard to explain, but it gives me the creeps."

"It's a scary play, Bree," Megan said, shrugging her shoulders. "Giving people the creeps is what it's supposed to do."

"Yeah, but it's supposed to give the *audience* the creeps," Bree pointed out. "Not the actors. I've had a nagging feeling that something isn't totally right with the play. Then Tiffany told us that story." Even mentioning the story sent a shiver through her.

"Story?" Megan asked, leaning in towards her sister.

Bree recounted the tale of the play as it had been performed thirty years earlier and the death of the girl playing the lead.

"And then last night I had a dream about it," she said, finishing her story. "And I saw it happen, Megan. I was right there, sitting in the front row when the light fell down on that girl. It seemed so real."

"Sounds to me like that play is *really* getting to you," Megan said. Bree thought that her sister almost sounded glad. "You know, some people just aren't cut out for the theatre. There's no shame in that. Maybe acting isn't for you."

"Thanks for being so sympathetic," Bree snapped, shoving her chair away from the table. "You're a big help."

She stormed back up to her room to get dressed. *That's the last time I go to her with my problems,* she thought. *I'm just going to get through this play and everything is going to be fine. It was just a dream. That's all. A dream.*

At school that day, Bree felt more focused than she had in a long time. The dream faded from her mind, and she didn't think about the play at all.

When the last bell rang, Bree hurried to the assembly hall for rehearsal with a renewed sense of purpose. After her fight with Megan that morning, she had managed to push aside her uneasy feeling about the play and was once again excited about playing Carrie.

"You look positively perky," Melissa said as she and Bree headed to the stage.

"Perky, huh?" Bree echoed. She decided not to tell Melissa about her dream, preferring to forget it. "I guess I have been a bit serious about all this. I let that story Tiffany told us get to me, but I know she was just making up all that stuff about it being cursed to get me to quit. This is just a play."

"Uh-huh," Melissa said, looking at her friend a bit strangely. "Right, and this is just a stage, and this is just a chair, and this is—"

"OK, OK," Bree said, sighing. "Never mind."

Ms Hollows hurried into the assembly hall.

"All right, ladies and gentlemen," she announced. "Let's run the Carrie and Rachel scene, please."

Bree was thrilled to notice that the set for Carrie's room was looking more like a real room than it had the day before. The set decorators had added more touches. Clothes, books and general junk were strewn everywhere around the room. A few old, worn-out sleeping bags were arranged in a circle on the floor. *A complete mess*, Bree thought. *Perfect for the scene of a haunted sleepover.*

"Ooh, the sleeping bags are here," Melissa cooed

when she stepped onto the stage. "Now it looks like a sleepover!"

The scene they were about to rehearse featured only Carrie and Rachel. Bree was thrilled to be alone on the stage with her real-life best friend. They walked onstage, and Bree immediately let herself be transported into character. She was no longer Bree, she was Carrie. Melissa was no longer Melissa, she was Rachel. This was not the stage in the assembly hall, it was Carrie's bedroom.

(RACHEL RUSHES TO CARRIE'S BEDROOM. CARRIE IS PACING, OBVIOUSLY UPSET.)

RACHEL: All right, Carrie. Spill it! What was so urgent that it couldn't wait?

CARRIE: Remember when I told you that I thought someone was following me?

RACHEL: Uh, yeah. It was just yesterday.

CARRIE: Right. Well, it happened again. Only now, it's happening everywhere.

RACHEL: What do you mean, EVERYWHERE?

CARRIE: Every time I walk down the corridors, I can feel someone following me. On every walk home from school, I'm certain I can hear footsteps behind me but no one is there. Even when I go from one room in my house to another, I feel it.

RACHEL: Hold on. Hold on. You "feel" someone following you. I'm not sure I know what that means. Have you actually seen anyone?

CARRIE: I hear footsteps all the time, and when I turn around, no one is there. But I know it, Rachel. I just know it! And what's worse--

RACHEL: There's a worse part?

CARRIE: I'm positive that whoever is following me means to do me harm!

Walking towards the front of the stage, still fully in character, Bree heard a snapping sound from above. She really didn't want to break out of her character, but something told her to look up, even though it wasn't in the script.

Glancing towards the track of stage lights above her, Bree saw that one of the lights had broken off and was plunging right towards her.

CHAPTER 7

Bree flung herself out of the way. She landed hard on her shoulder, just as the light crashed to the stage floor.

"Bree, are you all right?" Melissa screamed, dashing to her friend's side.

Ms Hollows and the entire cast rushed onto the stage.

"Gabrielle, are you all right?" Ms Hollows asked calmly.

Adrenaline shot through Bree's body. She felt numb. The shock of what had just happened, and what had *almost* happened made her feel as if time was standing still. She could see the stage light snap, then fall through the air in super-slow motion. The moment, stretched out over several seconds, replayed over and over in her mind. She saw the light hit the stage and explode into a million shards of glass. The slow-motion scene stopped, and time accelerated back to normal.

"I'm OK," Bree said, pushing herself up into a sitting position. Her mind began to clear as the shock wore off. Her shoulder was a bit sore, but as she got to her feet she realised that she had not been seriously injured. She hadn't even been hit by any glass.

"How could that have happened?" Melissa asked Ms Hollows in an almost accusatory tone. She peered up into the darkness of the catwalks and metal pipes that ran above the stage, but saw nothing and no one. By now the set decorators were running around, checking all the props. Everyone else was chattering about what had just happened and where they were when the light fell. Ms Hollows stood in the middle of all this chaos, eerily calm.

"What was that noise? I heard a . . ." Tiffany said as she walked out onto the stage from the wings and spotted the smashed-up light and the crowd surrounding Bree. "What happened?"

Bree stared at Tiffany and wondered where she had just been. Why hadn't she rushed onstage with everyone else? What had she been doing? Then Bree caught herself.

What am I thinking? Even she wouldn't try to hurt me ...
would she?

"I'm fine," Bree replied. "It was just an accident. Let's try that scene again. This time without the falling light."

Bree's little joke broke the tension onstage. "Fantastic, Gabrielle," Ms Hollows said. "The show must go on!"

A few minutes later the caretaker had cleaned up the broken light and the rehearsal resumed. This time the scene between Carrie and Rachel went off without a hitch.

When rehearsal ended, Bree and Melissa walked from the assembly hall, heading towards the front door of the school.

"So, Lis, I wasn't going to tell you about this, but after what happened today ..." Bree's words trailed off.

"Go on," Melissa encouraged her friend.

"Last night I had a terrifying dream," Bree began. "I was sitting in the audience of a theatre when I realised that it was actually our assembly hall. Then a play began, and it turned out to be *The Last Sleepover*."

"So you were dreaming about us doing the show," Melissa said, sounding a bit relieved to learn that her friend's big news was only about a dream.

"But that's just it, Lis," Bree continued. "It wasn't *us*

doing the show. In the dream everybody was wearing out-of-date clothes, like from the eighties or something. Then the girl playing Carrie came out onto the stage to start the show, and *she* was wearing those same kind of clothes. I think I was watching the original performance – the one that Tiffany told us about."

"Just because of the clothes?" Melissa asked. "I mean, dreams can be pretty weird. Your brain takes stuff from a bunch of different places and mashes it all up together."

"Not just the clothes, Lis," Bree said, taking a deep breath. "I saw the accident Tiffany described. I was sitting in the audience, watching the light fall onto the girl who was playing Carrie. It was just like Tiffany had described it. And it was exactly like what almost happened to me."

"So what are you saying, Bree?" Melissa asked. "That there's some evil spirit connected to the play? Or that someone is out to get you? I think Tiffany made up that story, and it's getting to you. I mean, if a girl died right here on this stage, then everyone would know about it, right?"

Bree nodded.

"And the light falling today?" Melissa added. "Well, that was just a coincidence. Accidents happen. Even coincidental ones."

Bree kept nodding. It was easier this way. Melissa made some good points, but that didn't explain away her uneasiness.

"Listen, I've got to go," Melissa continued. "My mum is picking me up. Are you sure you're OK? Do you want a lift home?"

"Nah, I'm going to stick around here for a bit," Bree said. She stood in the corridor and watched Melissa hurry from the school. Maybe Melissa was right. The whole thing – Tiffany's story, her dream, the accident at rehearsal – might be just a combination of made-up story and wild coincidence, but somehow she didn't believe that. She was still very shaken up.

Bree knew that because this was a Thursday, Mr Harris, the school librarian, stayed late to help pupils with their research projects. She turned towards the school library and marched down the corridor, striding purposefully. She would get to the bottom of all this. And she would do it now, before another rehearsal took place.

Bree opened the library's large oak door and walked inside. Every time she came here she realised just how lucky she was. She had seen a few other school libraries while visiting friends, but the library at Moorwood Secondary School was clearly a cut above.

She had almost forgotten how busy the place got on Thursdays after school. It had been a while since she'd had to come here for a research project.

Almost at the moment she entered the room, a short man with a thick shock of snow-white hair appeared from between two tall bookshelves and shuffled towards Bree.

"Bree Hart. How are you?" the man said.

"Hi, Mr Harris," Bree said. "I'm fine, thanks."

Seeing Mr Harris always made Bree smile. He had been at the school for more than twenty years. He loved his job, and though he'd long been eligible for retirement, he saw no reason to stop. This library, its books, computers and vast archives, was the focus of his life. And he loved nothing more than helping pupils.

"I haven't seen you in a while," Mr Harris said. "Now what can I help you with today?"

"I need to look into a bit of Moorwood Secondary School history," she replied.

"Ah, one of my favourite topics, since I've been here for most of it!" Mr Harris joked. "What are you looking for in particular?"

"Well, Mr Harris, I'm in the school play," Bree began.

"Yes, I know," the librarian said. "Playing the lead, if I'm not mistaken. I'm very much looking forward to seeing it."

"Yes," Bree continued, feeling a bit self-conscious. Until this moment she had been so focused on her work in the play that the thought of people she knew coming to see her perform hadn't crossed her mind in a while. "I'm actually here to research the history of the play itself. I believe it was performed at the school once before and only for one night."

"I see," Mr Harris said, his curiosity clearly piqued. "That was a little before my time, and now that you mention it, I do recall hearing about some incident related to a play. Do you know why the play was performed only once?"

"Well, that's what I'm here to find out," Bree explained. "I heard a story about what happened back then, but I wanted to find out whether or not it was really true."

"To quote a cliché, 'you've come to the right place'," Mr Harris said.

Bree could almost see an actual twinkle in his eye. He loved his work, and a new project, digging around, doing what he liked to call "informational archaeology", always made his face light up.

"I have every issue ever published of the school newsletter, dating from the beginning of the school's opening," Mr Harris explained. "Follow me, Bree."

Bree trailed a few steps behind him as he wended his way through the stacks. She always marvelled at how he seemed to know exactly where every single thing in this vast library could be found. And she had to walk at a fairly brisk pace to keep up with Mr Harris, who was well into his sixties. Once he was on the trail of information needed to solve a problem or answer a question, he wasted no time.

"Here we are," he said, practically hopping onto a small stepladder at the base of a tall bookcase. "When did you say the play was performed?"

"I don't have an exact year, Mr Harris, but I think it was about thirty years ago, so the early 1980s? The play is called *The Last Sleepover*."

Mr Harris ran his finger along the wide spines of row after row of plastic magazine holders. Each container held a year's worth of the monthly school newspaper. "Let's begin with 1979," he said, handing a container down to Bree. She placed it onto the desk beside the shelf. "Here's 1980, 1981 and 1982."

He stepped down from the ladder. Much to Bree's surprise, he took a seat beside her at the desk.

"I can do this myself if you have other pupils to help," she said, flattered by the special attention but a bit confused.

"Oh, anyone who needs help can find me," Mr Harris replied, his eyes sparkling. "I'm a bit of a theatre buff myself. And you know how much I love school history. Why don't you start with 1979, and I'll take 1980."

Bree took the container labelled SCHOOL NEWSLETTER – 1979 and pulled out the yellowed issues. She was immediately struck by the fashion and hairstyles of the pupils in the photos. Everyone looked as if they had stepped out of her dream.

Bree went issue by issue, carefully flipping through the delicate pages, scanning the paper for any mention of *The Last Sleepover*.

"It's not 1979," she said, when she had gone through the December issue.

"Nor is it 1980," Mr Harris added. He handed 1981 to Bree and took 1982 for himself.

Bree repeated the searching process with the issues from 1981. When she reached March, her eyes opened wide. "Mr Harris, here it is!" she cried, then looked around to see if she had disturbed anyone in the library.

Mr Harris pulled his chair up close to Bree's. She pointed to the page, then read the headline aloud: "'This Year's School Play Announced.'" She continued reading: "'The Drama department has decided that this year's show will be a brand-new play called *The Last Sleepover*. The play was written by and will be directed by Moorwood Drama teacher Mildred P. Wormhouse.'"

Bree paused. "Mildred!" she muttered to herself. "Millie is short for Mildred!" *Mildred P. Wormhouse, the playwright, must have named the ghost after herself. Was she a girl who never got invited to a sleepover?*

"Excuse me?" Mr Harris said.

"Huh, oh, I'm sorry, never mind, that name just made me think of something," Bree replied. She continued reading: "'The first meeting of all pupils interested in being involved with the play will be held on the 8th March in the assembly hall.'"

Bree set March aside and pulled out the April issue. She unfolded the paper and there, running across the front page, was a headline twice as big as any she had seen so far: LEAD ACTRESS DIES ON OPENING NIGHT.

CHAPTER 8

"So it's true!" Bree cried. "The story Tiffany told me is true!"

"Tiffany O'Brian?" Mr Harris asked.

"Yes," Bree replied, trying to regain her composure. "She's in the play with me. She told me that the girl playing the lead back then died in an accident on opening night."

"Hmm," Mr Harris said, thinking aloud. "I remember some hushed whispers about a girl who had died at the school, but I never got the full story. None of the older teachers ever wanted to talk about it, and they're all retired now. This happened ten years before I arrived at Moorwood. What does the article say?"

Bree started reading: "'Tragedy struck on the opening night of the school play when a stage light fell and killed

Year 7 pupil Gabrielle Ashford, who was playing the lead role in the play *The Last Sleepover*.'"

Bree stopped reading. *Gabrielle! The girl who died was named Gabrielle.*

"Bree?"

"I'm sorry, Mr Harris, I got lost in thought for a moment."

Bree continued reading: "Playwright, director and Moorwood Drama teacher Mildred P. Wormhouse was quoted as saying, 'The entire cast and crew are devastated. Working on this play, we became a family, and I could not have imagined anyone bringing the character I wrote to life any better than Gabrielle did. Our hearts go out to her friends and family.'"

Bree fell back into her seat.

"Are you all right?" Mr Harris asked.

"I'm – I'm OK, Mr Harris, thanks," Bree assured him. "This is all just so freaky. The play hasn't been performed since then. Until now. And I'm playing the lead, just like Gabrielle Ashford. And my name is Gabrielle."

"I don't think I've ever heard anyone at this school call you by your real first name," Mr Harris said.

"No, and there's only one person who does. Thank you

so much, Mr Harris. I really appreciate your help. I have to head home now."

"It's my pleasure, Bree. And come back anytime. It's always nice to see you."

"Thanks." Bree hurried from the library, her mind racing.

Mildred is Millie the ghost. Gabrielle is me. I mean, Gabrielle played the lead and died. Tiffany's story was true. She also said the play was cursed and that I would die. Is that true too?

"I've got to talk to Ms Hollows," Bree murmured to herself, heading to the assembly hall.

She shoved open the big assembly hall door and stepped inside. She saw no one.

"Ms Hollows!" she called out. "I need to talk to you." Her voice echoed around the empty, cavernous room. "Ms Hollows!" she yelled again, heading down the centre aisle towards the stage. Again she got no answer.

Bree bounded up the stairs leading onto the stage and scooted backstage. It too was empty. She was completely alone in the assembly hall. Or was she?

She got the strong feeling that someone was watching her. "Hello?" she called. "Is anybody here?"

Stop making yourself nuts, Bree, she thought as she

marched back up the aisle towards the door. *Go home. Get some rest. You are imagining …*

She spun around on her heels, certain that she would see someone behind her. The feeling of being watched was overwhelming. But she was alone.

Leaving the assembly hall, she strode quickly along the long corridor. She headed for the front door of the school, her footsteps echoing down the empty corridor. As Bree listened to the sound of her own footsteps, she could swear that she heard a second set of footsteps mingling with her own. She stopped.

Silence.

Resuming her walking, she heard the second set of steps again. This time she stopped and spun around. She saw no one.

Reaching the front door of the school, Bree glanced back over her shoulder one more time as she grabbed the door handle. This time she caught a glimpse of a shadow disappearing around a corner. She threw open the door, burst from the school, and ran home as fast as she could.

As she ran, above the sound of her own hard breathing, Bree heard footsteps following her the whole way home.

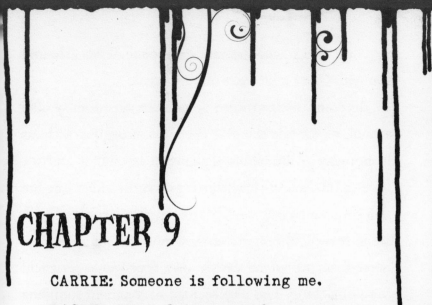

CHAPTER 9

CARRIE: Someone is following me.

RACHEL: What do you mean?

CARRIE: I heard footsteps behind me as I was walking home.

RACHEL: Did you see anyone at all?

CARRIE: No, that's what I'm saying. I didn't see anyone. But I did have the strong feeling that someone was following me, AND I clearly heard footsteps behind me. When I took a step, whoever was following me took a step. When I stopped, the second set of footsteps stopped.

RACHEL: Sometimes having a good imagination can be a problem, you know.

CARRIE: It's not my imagination. Something strange is happening.

"Cut! Very good scene, everyone," Ms Hollows shouted. "Let's take a ten-minute break."

Bree and Melissa were up onstage on Monday after school, rehearsing the play. Bree was struggling with her lines today – she hadn't slept again last night and was finding the lack of sleep starting to really affect her. She also found it a bit weird that they were rehearsing the scene in which Carrie thinks someone is following her home from school, so shortly after Bree had experienced the same thing. The play seemed determined to mirror her life – or was it the other way around?

And the events in the play seemed all the more real to Bree now that the set was completed. She caught the eye of Justin, the boy in charge of putting the set together. He was being extra cautious since the light incident and came out on the stage in between scenes to make sure everything was in order. Or in the case of the mess that was Carrie's bedroom, disorder.

"Everything looks great, Justin!" Bree said, trying to take her mind off things and focus on the fact that this was going to be a very good play.

"Thanks," Justin replied, tightening a clamp that held two sections of wall together. "It does look pretty cool."

"Now that the window is in, it looks like a real room."

"Check this out," Justin said, slipping back behind the wall in which the window hung. "Tony, do the lightning!"

Lights flashed on and off behind the window. The shutters whipped back and forth, slamming against the outside of the "house" as if the wind were blowing them during a storm.

"Very cool!" Bree exclaimed. "It's going to be great when an audience sees it."

"And we got the chandelier up and working," Justin said.

Bree glanced up and saw that the chandelier had been hung. It was dusty and covered with cobwebs. Its lights flickered on and off. She was standing directly beneath it.

A wave of fear suddenly swept through her as she relived the moment when the stage light fell right next to her. She took a step to the side so that she was no longer right under the fixture.

"Awesome," she said, regaining her composure.

Bree walked to the side of the stage, where she spotted the top of a staircase that the crew had built. The handrails and the top few stairs disappeared behind a curtain offstage, giving the impression that a person could walk downstairs to a lower level of the house.

"This looks so real!" Bree exclaimed, gripping the handrails and looking down, almost expecting to see a real staircase. Instead she saw a soft mattress a foot below, there to break her fall in the play's final scene. "You guys are good!"

Melissa, who had run off to the dressing room after their scene, joined Bree onstage.

"Doesn't it look incredible, Lis?" Bree asked.

"It's so real I'm almost scared!" Melissa joked.

Bree smiled, but Melissa's innocent comment reminded her of what had happened last week. She had tried to forget it. She didn't want to ever tell Melissa about it, but now she felt like she couldn't keep it to herself any longer. She pulled Melissa away from everyone and spoke in a voice barely above a whisper.

"This is going to sound so strange, but last Thursday, before I went home, I heard footsteps."

"Footsteps?"

"Yes. Well, first I thought that someone else was in the assembly hall."

"Well, that sounds terrifying," Melissa said sarcastically.

"It was actually because no one else *was* in the assembly hall. At least not that I could tell. And it felt like someone was watching me. Then, as I walked down the corridor towards the front door, I was certain I heard another set of footsteps. Someone was following me. I could just tell."

"Uh, we're on a break, Bree. No need to continue rehearsing."

"No joke, Lis," Bree said, realising as she said it how crazy this all sounded ... and how much like the lines they had just rehearsed. "I'm not talking as Carrie now. I'm me. And I'm telling you that the same thing that happens to Carrie in the show happened to me the other day. Someone followed me home."

"Did you see anyone?" Melissa asked.

"Not exactly."

"What do you mean, 'not exactly'? You either saw someone or you didn't."

"I caught glimpses, a quick peek of something, like a shadow moving in the corridor."

"Bree, I think this creepy play is really starting to get to you," Melissa said. "All this so-called crazy stuff can be easily chalked up to coincidence."

"But here's the other thing," Bree continued. "I went to the library and found out that the girl playing Carrie thirty years ago did die on opening night. And, get this. Her name was Gabrielle!"

"Yeah, so . . ."

"Don't you see, Lis? It's all happening again. It's connected. There's something not right about this whole play. Tiffany was right!"

"Say it louder. I love when people say that," Tiffany said, stepping up behind Bree. "What was I right about?"

"The girl who died thirty years ago," Bree replied. "How'd you know?"

"Something I overheard my parents talking about ages ago. I told you the play was haunted," Tiffany said. "You should quit before something happens."

"Are you threatening her?" Melissa asked.

"I'm just saying," Tiffany replied casually, walking away.

"I can't believe she's still trying to get your part," Melissa said, seemingly more upset at Tiffany's words than Bree was.

"I'm starting to wonder exactly what I believe, Lis," Bree said softly, not quite sure if Melissa even heard her.

"OK, everyone, the break is over," Ms Hollows announced. "Places onstage, please."

Once again, Bree tried her best to shrug off her unease and put her mind back into the play.

The girls took their places for a key scene in the show. In the story, the sleepover was well underway. Carrie suggests they play a game.

> CARRIE: The game is called "The Witch's Body". It's a bit creepy and a bit goofy.
>
> (CARRIE PULLS OUT A LARGE PLASTIC BAG BULGING WITH ITEMS INSIDE IT.)
>
> CARRIE: This is the story of the witch who was so old that her body began to fall apart. And it just so happens that I've got the body parts right here in this bag!
>
> (CARRIE SHAKES THE BAG MENACINGLY AT HER FRIENDS. THE OBJECTS RATTLE AND MAKE SQUISHING SOUNDS.)
>
> RACHEL: Body parts? Gross!
>
> CARRIE: That's where the game part comes in. I'm going to pick a body part from this bag and put it in this smaller bag.
>
> (CARRIE TAKES A SMALL PLASTIC BAG AND PUTS IT NEXT TO THE LARGER BAG.)
>
> CARRIE: Everyone will take a turn reaching into the small bag and

feeling a body part. Then you have to say what body part it is and what the object REALLY is. OK, now, everyone close your eyes.

(CARRIE REACHES INTO THE LARGE BAG AND PULLS OUT ONE OF THE ITEMS. THEN SHE PUTS IT INTO THE SMALL BAG.)

RACHEL: I'll go first!

(RACHEL SHOVES HER HAND INTO THE BAG.)

RACHEL: EWW! I feel something round and wet and squishy. And it's bigger than my hand. Wait. Wait. I know. It's the witch's heart!

CARRIE: You got it. OK, now what is it really?

RACHEL: A - a peeled tomato!

CARRIE: Two points for Rachel. OK, Laura, you're up.

(SOUND EFFECT: TAP. TAP. TAP. THE GIRLS ARE ALL STARTLED BY A TAPPING NOISE AT THE WINDOW.)

RACHEL: What was that?

LAURA: Sounded like someone tapping on the window.

CARRIE: Yeah, but we're on the first floor. How could someone be up here?

LAURA: Maybe it was just the wind blowing a tree branch against the window.

CARRIE: Totally. Let's get back to the game.

(CARRIE PULLS ANOTHER "BODY PART" FROM THE BIG BAG AND PUTS IT INTO THE SMALL ONE. LAURA REACHES INTO THE BAG.)

LAURA: I feel two little round squishy things. I know. I've got the witch's eyeballs.

CARRIE: Great!

LAURA: And I know what they really are. They're peeled grapes!

CARRIE: Another two points. Excellent. I--

(SOUND EFFECT: TAP! TAP! TAP!)

CARRIE: Did you see it? Did you see it?

RACHEL: See what?

CARRIE: The face! There was a face in the window.

(LIGHTNING FLASHES, REVEALING THE FACE OF A LITTLE GIRL WITH DARK, SUNKEN EYES AT THE WINDOW. CARRIE IS THE ONLY ONE TO SEE IT.)

CARRIE: Look!

(ALL HEADS TURN TOWARDS THE WINDOW, BUT WHEN THE LIGHTNING ILLUMINATES THE OUTSIDE, THERE IS NO FACE AT THE WINDOW.)

RACHEL: So now you're seeing things?

CARRIE: Seeing things? You all saw the hairbrush and the mirror, right? And I saw her face.

LAURA: The ghost.

CARRIE: Yes, the gh--

(THERE ARE TAPPING SOUNDS AGAIN AT THE WINDOW. THIS TIME THEY ARE EVEN LOUDER AND MORE URGENT. EVERYONE TURNS BACK TO THE WINDOW. THERE, STARING IN AT THEM FROM OUTSIDE, IS THE GHOST.)

EVERYONE: YIIEEE!

(THE GIRLS ALL SCREAM AND RUSH TO THE SIDE OF CARRIE'S BEDROOM OPPOSITE THE WINDOW, TRYING TO GET AS FAR AWAY AS THEY CAN FROM IT. CARRIE'S BLACK CAT ARCHES ITS BACK AND HISSES.)

RACHEL: Who could it be? How did she get up here?

CARRIE: Either someone is pulling a prank ...

RACHEL: Or?

80

```
CARRIE: Or it's the ghost of the girl
who used to live in this house,
trying to come to our sleepover!
```

"And fade the lights to black," Ms Hollows said. "Excellent, girls. Gather around for notes. Can we have our ghost out onstage, please?"

Tiffany came walking out from backstage, still wearing her scary pale mask with black, soulless eyes. She joined the others at centre stage.

"Nice job, Tiffany," Melissa said as Tiffany sat down beside her. "But next time you should try the scene with the mask *on*."

"Very funny," Tiffany replied, pulling off the mask and scowling. "Maybe you should be in a comedy instead of a scary play."

"The ghost is an important character," Bree said.

"Don't placate me, *Gabrielle*," Tiffany shot back. "I know exactly what my role is in this production. I don't need your pity, and I don't need your pitiful attempts to try to make me feel better."

Bree turned away. She had tried being friendly to Tiffany at every rehearsal, even though it seemed at times as if Tiffany was trying to scare her into leaving the show. But enough was enough. She didn't like Tiffany. She didn't have to be her friend. She didn't have to make her feel better. She just had to work with her in the play.

Ms Hollows gave the cast their notes. She was very pleased with how the play was taking shape, but there were always things that needed to be tightened up and fine-tuned so that the play would go off without a hitch when it was performed in front of an audience.

Following notes, Ms Hollows dismissed the cast.

"I think Tiffany makes a great ghost, don't you?" Melissa asked Bree as the two left the school building.

"Why does she have to be so snotty all the time, Lis?"

"Hey, it just wouldn't be Tiffany without the attitude, now would it? Forget about her. With any luck, that mask will get stuck to her face and we won't have to listen to her whine any more. See you tomorrow, Bree. Got to run."

"See ya."

Arriving at home, Bree found a note from her parents:

> Out getting groceries with Megan. We'll
> be back in time for dinner. Snacks in the
> fridge.
>
> Love, M + D

She threw open the fridge door and pulled out a plate filled with cut-up pieces of fruit and a few biscuits, then headed for the stairs leading up to her bedroom.

Suddenly all the lights in the house began to flicker on and off.

What's going on? she wondered, pausing at the bottom of the staircase.

Again the lights flickered on and off. Then they went off and stayed off.

Placing the plate of snacks on a small table in the hallway, Bree opened a drawer at the front of the table and pulled out a torch. Her family kept torches handy in case of power cuts. But this was different.

She noticed that although every light in the house seemed to be out, they hadn't actually lost power. Digital clocks on the front of the coffeemaker in the kitchen and the DVR in the living room still glowed with the correct time. Only the lights seemed to be affected. Bree wondered if she somehow blew a fuse.

She flipped the hallway light switch on and off several times, but the lights stayed dark. Turning the torch on, she headed upstairs, thinking that maybe the lights up there would work. Reaching her room, she stepped in and tried the main light switch.

Nothing.

Then her bedside lamp.

Nothing.

Yet the numbers on her alarm clock still shone brightly.

Walking around her bedroom in the dark, carrying a torch, gave Bree a very creeped-out feeling. It was as if she were still walking around the stage in the dark, searching Carrie's bedroom with only a torch.

This is way too close to the play, she thought.

Bree swept the torch's beam across her wall. As the light passed the window, she spotted a face staring at her from outside. It had dark, sunken eyes.

CHAPTER 10

Moving exactly as she had just an hour earlier at rehearsal, Bree raced across the room, yanked the window open, and stuck her head out. But just as in the play, the face had vanished. Bree swept her torch down to the street. She leaned out of the window and shone the beam left, right, down, even up, searching for that haunting face. But it was officially gone.

All right. This is going too far, Bree thought. *Maybe I'm really Carrie, and this whole Bree thing is a part in a play.*

"Bree! We're home!" her dad called from downstairs.

"Pull yourself together," she murmured to herself as she raced from her room and bounded down the stairs, following the beam of her torch. As she ran, a thought popped into her head. Maybe she wasn't crazy after all.

"Megan!" Bree shouted, storming right up to her sister, putting her face nose-to-nose with Megan's. "Were you just outside my window? Are you trying to scare me out of doing the play?"

"Outside your window?" Megan asked incredulously. "How would I get up there?"

"What are you talking about?" her mother said sternly. "Your sister has been with us for the past two hours. She came into the house with us just now. And speaking of the house, why are you here in the dark?"

"All the lights just went out at the same time," Bree explained. "I tried—"

Flick!

Bree was interrupted by the sound of her mother flipping on the light switch – the same switch that Bree had flipped up and down lots of times just a few minutes earlier. The lights came right on.

"The lights work fine," her mother said. "Are you feeling all right?"

"I don't know about you, Mum, but it's clear to me that the pressure of doing this play is proving to be too much for poor Bree," Megan said, her voice positively dripping with condescension.

Their mother gave Megan a reproachful look, but she didn't say anything. Maybe she was starting to think Bree was cracking under the pressure too. And if she was being perfectly honest with herself, Bree was beginning to agree with her. She must have imagined the face in the window.

Normally she would have protested both the tone and content of Megan's comment. She would have whined to her mother about how Megan had been against her from the start, how her sister should be more supportive, and on and on.

But Megan was right. The pressure of the play, the weird connections between what happened in the story and what was happening in her life, were blurring the lines between where Carrie ended and where Bree began.

And thinking that, Bree finally came to a decision. Despite the fact that they were far into the rehearsal process, she would quit the play. Tomorrow.

Much to her surprise, she slept better that night than she had for a while. No bad dreams. No dreams of any kind that she could remember. The incident with the face in her window began to fade from her thoughts. Perhaps having made the decision to leave the play had calmed her mind, freed her from the craziness that had invaded her life ever since the moment she'd got the part in the show. Whatever it was, she awoke the next morning rested and refreshed.

"Any more scary faces at your window?" Megan asked, munching a piece of toast.

"The only scary face I see is the one opposite me now," Bree replied, feeling much more like sparring with her sister than she had the night before.

"Ha-ha, very funny," Megan replied. "But I still think you should quit that show before you completely lose all your marbles."

Bree just shrugged casually. Although she had made her decision, something in her mind told her not to say anything to Megan until the deed was actually done.

"Got to run," was all she said, tossing her napkin onto her plate and pushing her chair away from the table. "You'll be a dear and put these in the sink for me, won't you?"

Before Megan could reply, Bree jumped up from the table and ran towards the door.

"Mum!" Megan whined at the top of her voice.

"She left already," Bree called back to the kitchen. "Bye!" Then she scooted out of the door.

At the start of her classes, Bree felt confident about her decision. She imagined what she would say to Ms Hollows that afternoon. But as the day wore on, she grew more and more anxious about going into rehearsal and actually saying the words "I quit" aloud. By the time classes ended and Bree was walking to the assembly hall, she was practically in a state of panic. She opened the door to the assembly hall, stepped inside, and knew instantly that she wasn't going to quit the show.

There was something different about being in that theatre. As if the place, or more accurately, the play, had a life of its own. And Bree felt as if it had some influence over her life. She decided not to fight it and to simply hope things would get better. That the weird stuff would stop and that she could find a clearer line between Bree and Carrie. But at this point, could that actually happen?

"Let's pick up the scene, girls, just before Carrie gets the phone call, shall we?" Ms Hollows announced as the girls all took the stage.

RACHEL: So do you really think that was someone at your window?

CARRIE: I don't know what to think.

LAURA: Let's just try to forget about everything and go back to that Witch's Body game.

CARRIE: Good idea. My turn.

(SOUND EFFECT: BRIIIING! BRIIIING! BRIIIING! EVERYONE JUMPS AS THE PHONE IN CARRIE'S BEDROOM RINGS LOUDLY.)

CARRIE: Who in the world could be calling me? It's so late.

(CARRIE PICKS UP THE PHONE. A VOICE STARTS SPEAKING.)

FEMALE VOICE ON PHONE: Leave now, and never come back ... or you'll be sorry!

(CARRIE PRESSES THE SPEAKERPHONE BUTTON JUST AS THE MESSAGE REPEATS.)

FEMALE VOICE OVER SPEAKERPHONE: Leave now, and never come back ... or you'll be sorry!

(SOUND EFFECT: CLICK!)

RACHEL: That was one crazy prank call.

CARRIE: Something tells me it wasn't a prank call. I'm going to call them back.

(CARRIE DIALS THE NUMBER.)

OPERATOR'S VOICE FROM PHONE: The number you have dialled is not in service. No more information is available.

They ran the scene three times until Ms Hollows was happy with it. Bree felt herself dragging a bit. After rehearsal, she and Melissa stood outside the school.

"Rehearsal was a bit slow today, don't you think, Lis?" Bree asked.

"Seemed OK to me," Melissa said, shrugging. "But I guess Ms Hollows agreed with you, since she made us do the scene three times."

BRIIIING! BRIIIING! BRIIIING!

Bree's mobile rang. She jumped a bit, realising that it was ringing with the same old-fashioned ringtone that the sound effects engineer had chosen to use for Carrie's phone in the play.

Glancing down at her screen, she saw the caller ID: UNKNOWN NUMBER.

Bree pressed speakerphone.

A female with a hollow, distant voice said, "Leave now, and never come back . . . or you'll be sorry!"

CHAPTER 11

"It's got to be a prank, Bree," Melissa said when Bree had hung up the call. "Someone who was at rehearsal and saw the scene we just did."

"And who do you think that might be?" Bree said, not even trying to disguise the anger in her voice. "The voice was kind of familiar. I just can't exactly put my finger on it, but guess who is number one on my list?"

"Tiffany," Melissa answered. "You know, Bree, I thought you were being a little paranoid, suspecting that Tiffany was actively trying to get you to leave the play. But now, this seems like a no-brainer. She's still inside, you know."

"Come on," Bree said, charging back towards the front

door of the school. "I'm going to put a stop to this right now."

Bree threw open the front door and marched towards the assembly hall. Her sense of purpose was firm. She felt more committed to confronting Tiffany than she had felt about anything since her involvement in the play began. Maybe if she could get Tiffany to stop trying to make her quit, everything would be better. Everything might actually feel normal again.

Reaching the assembly hall, with Melissa close on her heels, Bree burst through the doors and stomped down the aisle towards the stage. Tiffany stood at the edge of the stage, packing up her things and getting ready to go home.

"Tiffany!" Bree boomed.

"Well, if it isn't the star," Tiffany replied, smirking. "What's got you all in an uproar?"

"*You*, that's what!" Bree shouted. "It's got to stop, Tiffany! The other night it was the face at the window – did you use the mask from the play to do that? And now the phone calls! Enough!" Bree was amazed at herself. She had never felt so angry in her life. She felt as if she were watching another person explode in fury, blaming Tiffany for everything that had happened.

"What are you talking about?" Tiffany replied, dropping her smirking, above-it-all act, seeming to be genuinely startled by the blast of anger she had just received from the usually meek and mild Bree.

"Tell me you didn't just call my mobile and say the same words that Carrie hears on her phone in the play," Bree demanded.

"Uh, OK, I didn't just call your mobile and say the same—"

"I don't believe you, Tiffany!" Bree shouted. "Why don't you show me your phone? Show me what your last outgoing call was."

"I think that being in this play has made you crack," said Tiffany, unknowingly echoing the sentiments of Bree's sister. She opened the zip to the front compartment of her backpack, pulled out her mobile phone, and thrust it towards Bree.

"Here. Knock yourself out," she said as Bree snatched the phone from her hand.

Bree scrolled through the "call history" menu until she got to "recent calls made". The last call Tiffany had made was to MUM.

"Happy?" Tiffany asked, grabbing her phone back. "I

called my mum a couple of minutes ago to tell her I was leaving rehearsal and heading home. So I don't know what you're talking about."

Bree looked at Melissa, who shrugged.

That was when Bree's phone rang again.

BRIIIING! BRIIIING! BRIIIING!

Again the caller ID read UNKNOWN NUMBER.

Bree looked at Tiffany, who was standing right next to Melissa. Tiffany had already put her phone away. Bree answered the call.

"Leave now, and never come back … or you'll be sorry!" said the female with the same familiar voice.

"Who *is* this?" Bree screamed into the phone. She got no reply.

It was now clear that it could not have been Tiffany who had been making the calls. Tiffany was standing right next to her. Bree's mind flashed on Megan for a moment, as she ran through a list of people who didn't want her to be in the show. But she knew that Megan had band practice at this time, and mobile phones were strictly forbidden.

So who is it? Who is calling me with a warning? And should I listen to her?

CHAPTER 12

Bree decided to walk home. She could have taken the bus or called her mum for a lift, but she needed some time alone. She often did some of her best thinking on long walks, and this one might just help her sort out her thoughts.

Then again, it might not.

For what felt like the millionth time, Bree ran through the details of everything that had been happening and everything that she had been feeling since she first got involved with the play. She felt almost as if there were two different people living inside her head – normal Bree, who had simply decided that she wanted to break out of her shell and be in a play, and then another Bree.

Normal Bree was the one who had been determined to stay in the play no matter what, just to prove her sister wrong. But that was also the Bree who was beginning to feel that she should leave the play, despite any ridicule she might get from Megan or Tiffany or anyone else, when crazy things started to happen, like lights falling on her or seeing faces in windows. That Bree was practical and usually trusted her feelings. If that had been the only Bree, she would have left the play, no question.

Then there was the feeling of being drawn to the play as if it had some magical power over her. As if she were under some kind of spell. That Bree was the one who'd lost it on Tiffany as the other Bree, normal Bree, watched as if she were indeed another person.

That was it! That was the problem. It was all clear to her now. It was the two-Bree situation.

The two-Bree situation? she thought, frowning. *You really are losing your mind.*

As she approached her house, she realised that although she had clarified a few things, she still had no explanation for the phone calls or other mysterious things. *So I'm right back where I started,* she thought. *Still in the play.*

Still wanting to quit the play. Still not going to quit the play. Dealing with two "Brees" arguing in my head.

That night at dinner Bree eyed Megan suspiciously. Logic told her that Megan could not have been the one making those calls, yet somehow she felt she couldn't trust her sister.

"So how're rehearsals going?" Megan asked.

Bree was startled. Was this really her sister being friendly, showing interest in her, making small talk? Maybe someone had taken over part of *her* brain too, and now there was a nice Megan living in there along with the usual self-centred one.

"OK, I guess," Bree replied cautiously. The last person in the world she would confide in regarding all this craziness was Megan. "I'm remembering all my lines, and I like being onstage with the other kids. I think the show is going to be OK."

"Great!" Megan replied, getting up from the table. "I can't wait to see it."

"You're going to come and see the show?" Bree asked incredulously.

"Of course. Wouldn't miss it!"

Bree couldn't help smiling. *There is definitely someone else* living in that head of hers. *I just hope that "nice Megan" sticks around for a while*, she thought.

After dinner, Bree went to her room and dived into her homework. She found it surprisingly easy to focus. She had always been a good student. Now she was using schoolwork to help get her mind off the play and relax.

As she finished her homework, she got a text from Melissa. ANY MORE WEIRD PHONE CALLS? MAYBE YOU SHOULD CHANGE YOUR NUMBER!

Bree wrote back. NOPE. TRYING TO FORGET ALL THAT. CAN'T WAIT UNTIL THE PLAY IS DONE. I'LL BE HAPPY WHEN MY LIFE RETURNS TO ITS NORMAL BORING SELF!

Melissa replied instantly. WELL, YOU ONLY HAVE TWO MORE DAYS TO DEAL WITH IT. G-NITE!

G-NITE!

Melissa was right. Opening night was just a couple of days away now. Bree really was entering the home stretch of this whole strange experience. Soon it would all be behind her – both the good parts and the creepy ones.

After reading for a while, she started to feel drowsy, the stress of the day – the past two weeks, in fact – catching up with her. She fell into a deep sleep, then tumbled into the most vivid nightmare she had ever had.

In the dream, the idea of "two Brees" came stunningly alive. She felt herself floating in the air, looking down – on herself!

She couldn't tell if she was actually flying or just seeing the world from a new point of view. But since this was a dream, it didn't really matter. The laws of nature and physics had no meaning here. All she knew was that she was able to watch herself, as if she were in the high balcony of a theatre, watching her life like a play. And the odd thing was, this new perspective felt perfectly normal, as if it were an everyday experience that people had all the time.

Bree watched herself wake up and slip out of bed.

Is my room really that messy?

She watched as she ate breakfast silently beside Megan, who seemed to be completely self-absorbed.

Looks like the "real" Megan showed up for breakfast.

Bree was unable to shake the feeling that she was simply watching a play. Actually it was more like a movie, as the scene shifted from her house to school. She had a perfect view of herself as she continued to look down from above.

She watched herself walk to school. The closer she got to the building, the more her sense of wonderment at this new point of view on her life lessened. It was replaced by dread, as if something terrible was going to happen at school. She knew it, yet she was powerless to stop it. With each step she took, the anxiety grew more and more overbearing.

As she watched herself stepping into the school, a sense of evil and impending doom washed over her.

Stop! she thought, hoping that maybe she could command this "show" to end, as if she were pressing the stop button on a remote. But the "show" continued. She did not wake up, and images of her life did not stop playing out in front of her eyes.

She watched herself go through her day of lessons. The slight thrill of "spying" on her own life, which she had enjoyed at first, vanished. All she could think about was how to turn the images off, how to stop herself from stepping into whatever she was certain was going to happen.

When classes ended, Bree watched herself walk through the corridors on her way to the assembly hall for rehearsal. Her dread ratcheted up to a new intensity as the Bree below grabbed the handle and opened the assembly hall door.

Once inside, rehearsal of the final scene proceeded smoothly.

(THE GIRLS ARE OUT OF THEIR SLEEPING BAGS, PACING AROUND THE ROOM NERVOUSLY.)

CARRIE: This is not how I pictured my sleepover going.

RACHEL: Well, I don't believe in ghosts either, but what else could it be?

CARRIE: I know. What other explanation could there be? It all adds up - the girl who died, the face at the window, the floating objects--

LAURA: Don't forget the phone calls.

CARRIE: Ghosts making phone calls?

LAURA: I know how it sounds, but why is it stranger than ghosts doing any of the other things?

RACHEL: Why don't you just invite her to the sleepover and be done with it?

CARRIE: No, she is not welcome. She's a ghost. She's not one of us. She's not even alive. There's no way she's coming to my sleepover!

LAURA: Uh ... I think you should tell HER that!

(LAURA POINTS OVER CARRIE'S SHOULDER. EVERYONE TURNS AROUND AND GASPS IN HORROR AS THEY SEE THE GHOST WALKING INTO THE ROOM, HEADING RIGHT TOWARDS CARRIE.)

CARRIE: Get out! You are not welcome here!

(THE GHOST IGNORES CARRIE AND CONTINUES TO WALK TOWARDS HER. CARRIE BACKS AWAY, MOVING TOWARDS THE TOP OF THE STAIRS.)

RACHEL: Carrie, look out!

(CARRIE BACKS UP, RIGHT TO THE TOP OF THE STAIRS. THE GHOST IS VERY CLOSE TO HER NOW. CARRIE TAKES A FINAL STEP BACKWARD AND TUMBLES DOWN THE STAIRS, FALLING OFFSTAGE. THE LIGHTS GO TO BLACK.)

Laura and Rachel: YIIIIII!!!!!!

THE END

Bree was fascinated by watching the play as if she was part of the audience. She had seen plays before, certainly, but never one in which she was acting!

And she realised, oddly enough for the first time, here in her dream, why the play was called *The Last Sleepover*. All along she had thought the title referred to the ghost's last sleepover, but she was wrong.

This was the story of *Carrie's* last sleepover, as if the ghost had wanted something bad to happen to Carrie from the beginning. As if the ghost was blaming Carrie for having kept her away from all those sleepovers. Now, in the end, in the play, the ghost, Millie – Mildred P. Wormhouse – had got her revenge.

Bree watched as the cast ran through the entire play again. She guessed that this had to be one of the final rehearsals. Everyone was so prepared, doing the play exactly as they would on opening night.

"Excellent!" Ms Hollows said when the rehearsal was finished. "I have never felt more confident about a play I have been involved with."

"Opening night is tomorrow, ladies and gentlemen," Ms Hollows continued. "Everyone please get a good night's sleep. I will see all of you for the performance."

Wow! Opening night. I wonder if I'll—

Before Bree's dreaming mind could even complete the thought, the scene before her switched. She was still looking down at the assembly hall, only now it was filling up with people.

Her dream had shifted to opening night.

Bree spotted her parents and Megan, sitting right in the front row.

A hush fell over the audience as the houselights dimmed and the curtain went up. The stage lights came on, revealing the set for Carrie's bedroom.

A thrill ran through Bree. *Here I go! This is so exciting!*

She watched herself step out onto the stage. The audience applauded wildly. Perhaps the person clapping the loudest was her sister, Megan. A great feeling of satisfaction washed over her.

The audience grew quiet. Onstage Bree took a breath, then opened her mouth to start the show.

BOOOOOM!!!

A thunderous explosion rocked the assembly hall.

Now Bree saw herself buried onstage in a cloud of smoke and debris.

CHAPTER 13

Bree bolted upright in bed, covered in cold sweat. She tossed her covers onto the floor, then followed them off the bed. Landing on the pile of covers, she wrapped herself up like a cocoon, rocking back and forth on the floor. A few moments later she realised that she was whimpering like a baby. She felt out of control, as if her life had been taken away from her and all she could do was watch from the sidelines – or the balcony.

The dream she had just had was no ordinary nightmare. It was a warning. Whoever or whatever was now controlling her life was trying to tell her that something bad was going to happen if she walked out onto that stage on the opening night of this play.

Bree rolled onto her side and pushed herself up to a

standing position. Her path was now clear. She had to get dressed, go to school, and tell Ms Hollows that she could not do the play.

I know, I know, she began saying to herself, but in some ways it felt as if she were arguing with another person — more specifically, another Bree. *How can you do this? Opening night is tomorrow. You can't just walk out on everyone. The whole cast, all your friends, Ms Hollows — the whole school is depending on you to come through. How can you leave them in the lurch like that?*

"No!" Bree shouted, then caught herself, hoping no one else in the house had heard her. She lowered her voice as she continued the conversation. "I can't let what everybody else thinks control my life any more. That's one of the reasons I decided to do the play in the first place. Megan thought I wasn't cut out for the theatre. Tiffany thought I didn't deserve to have the lead in the play. And now, if everyone thinks I'm a quitter, well, that's just too bad! I don't care what everyone thinks. I don't even care what *you* think!"

She stopped, realising that she was now staring in the mirror, carrying on this argument with her reflection.

That sudden awareness acted like a splash of cold water in the face.

"Walk away from the mirror, Bree, eat a piece of toast, and go to school like a normal person."

But once again, on the walk to school, Bree's mind began to change. As if the school building – or more specifically, the assembly hall – exerted some force, some control, over her thoughts. The closer she got to the school, the stronger the feeling that compelled her to do the play in the first place got. By the time she walked into school, she knew that she was going to that afternoon's final rehearsal, and that she would indeed walk out onto the stage tomorrow night, opening night, and perform the part of Carrie.

None of which lessened her anxiety. She could not get the image of the explosion out of her mind. Through each lesson, walking in the corridors between lessons, sitting at lunch, and talking to her friends, she felt distracted, her mind locked on that single, devastating image.

"Earth to Bree," someone said as she walked through the corridor on her way to rehearsal.

Bree spun around, practically jumping into the air.

"Melissa!" she cried. "You shouldn't sneak up on

people." She tried to joke her way out of the reality that her mind was far away, lost in her terrible dream.

"You've been in a fog all day, Bree," Melissa said. "Getting the 'I can't believe opening night is tomorrow' jitters?"

"Maybe," Bree replied flatly. She had already told Melissa too many weird things. She was not about to share her most recent nightmare with her too.

"Are you kidding?" Melissa said. "Even with all the bizarre stuff you've had to deal with, you have been the glue that holds this show together, Bree. You're a rock. You are going to rule tomorrow night!"

If I survive, Bree thought, grimacing.

"Thanks, Lis," Bree said, trying to sound happy – like her usual self. "I guess it is opening-night nerves. What else could it be? I mean, this *is* my first play, and I am playing the lead."

"You'll be great," Melissa repeated as they reached the assembly hall. She pulled open the door, and Bree followed her inside.

"Ladies and gentlemen, please assemble onstage," Ms Hollows said as Bree reached the front of the assembly hall.

Bree joined the rest of the cast on the stage.

"This is our final rehearsal. Our dress rehearsal. We will be performing the entire play, start to finish, exactly as we will be doing it tomorrow night in front of an audience. Before we begin, I would like to let each and every one of you know that I could not be more proud of you," Ms Hollows began. "You started as a group of individuals, each with your own ideas about what this play was and what your part in it would be. In the weeks we have worked together, we have become a unit, a team. Each of you has put aside any notion you walked in here with, for the good of the play, and your performances certainly reflect that. I could not have asked for a better cast.

"Watching you bring the author's words to life has been a rewarding experience for me. I believe in this play strongly, as strongly as if I had written it myself. And on that note, let's begin. Break a leg, everyone!"

As the cast headed backstage, the lights dimmed, and Bree stepped out from behind the curtain to begin the first scene. As she opened her mouth to deliver her first line, a wave of panic seized her. The image of the explosion played out in front of her eyes, as if someone were projecting a film of her dream right here, where it happened.

"I – I," Bree stammered. She was Bree, alone and frightened on the stage. She was not in character at all. She was certainly not Carrie. She was Bree caught in the grip of the deadly vision that now haunted her every waking minute.

Ms Hollows stepped up to the edge of the stage. "Gabrielle," she said. "What is the problem?"

"I'm sorry, Ms Hollows," Bree said, using every bit of willpower to push aside the terror and the panic that shook her whole body. "Must just be nerves. Let's start again. I'll get it this time."

Bree walked offstage and took a deep breath. *You only have to do this a few more times in your entire life. You know the lines. You know what to do. Just do it!*

She walked back onto the stage. The lights dimmed, and this time she became Carrie. The play began, and she moved from scene to scene seamlessly. The further into the play she got, the more her sense of panic and impending doom eased.

She felt comfortable as Carrie.

It was even somewhat of a relief to lose herself in the

character, to become someone else for a couple of hours.

When the dress rehearsal had ended, Ms Hollows called the cast together. "Excellent! I have never felt more confident about a play I have been involved with. Opening night is tomorrow, ladies and gentlemen," she said. "Everyone please get a good night's sleep. I will see all of you for the performance."

A rush of all-too-familiar anxiety overwhelmed Bree. *Those are exactly the same words Ms Hollows said in my dream. And then ... and then ...*

All the calm and relief she had felt during the rehearsal vanished in a moment.

Struggling to hold herself together, Bree hurried backstage. She didn't want Melissa to see her like this. She didn't want anyone to see her like this. She just wanted it to all be over. The fear, the nightmares, the crazy masks and lights and phone calls, the play.

The play.

Ever since it had come into her life, Bree had felt as if the play was a really bad thing disguised as a really good thing.

Every time she had begun to feel good about the

experience, something inside, something deeper, felt off, wrong, even threatened. The play would be finished soon and she would be free – free of the power it seemed to hold over her. And then she would never have to do it again.

"Coming, Bree?" Melissa asked, sticking her head backstage.

"Nah, my mum's coming to pick me up," Bree said, trying her hardest to act normal. "I'll hang out here."

"'Kay," Melissa said. "See ya tomorrow for the big show!"

"Tomorrow," Bree repeated. Melissa left the assembly hall, along with the rest of the cast.

Bree knew that her mum would be there in about twenty minutes. Enough time to do what she needed to do. She hurried from the assembly hall and raced to the library, knowing it was unlocked. Slipping into the room, she was overwhelmed by the silence. It was so weird to be here without Mr Harris, and without a roomful of studying pupils. But she didn't need Mr Harris's help for this. She just needed a computer, and she couldn't wait until she got home to use her own.

Signing onto one of the library's computers, she

searched online for "Mildred P. Wormhouse". As she typed the name, she wondered why she hadn't done this earlier. It seemed to Bree that the key to all of this had to rest with the playwright herself.

After a few minutes of digging, she found a website dedicated to obscure playwrights. Searching through the names, she found what she was looking for – a short biography of Mildred P. Wormhouse.

Reading the bio, Bree learned that *The Last Sleepover* was the only play that Wormhouse ever wrote. Apparently, she had had a difficult, unhappy childhood. She had few friends and spent much time alone. The bio referred to the death of Gabrielle Ashford on the opening night of the play at Moorwood Secondary School. And it also said that Mildred P. Wormhouse apparently disappeared shortly after the event and was never heard from again.

Her whereabouts, or even whether she was still alive, remained unknown.

Wormhouse was quoted in the piece as saying, "I was endlessly tormented by one particular bully. As a matter of fact, she was the inspiration for my play. She turned everyone at school against me, and there was nothing I

114

could do about it. And so, since I had no control over events in my real life, I decided to get my revenge through my writing, through *The Last Sleepover*. Not to be too obvious, I shortened the name of the poor tormented ghost in my play from my own 'Mildred' to just 'Millie'. And I changed the name of my tormentor completely, calling her Carrie rather than her true name – Gabrielle."

Bree reached the end of the bio and sat, stunned. Not only was the girl who died thirty years named Gabrielle, but so was the bully who'd excluded young Mildred from sleepovers – the inspiration for the play itself.

"This whole play is about revenge," Bree said to herself. "Revenge against the Gabrielle who excluded Mildred. Was it also revenge against Gabrielle Ashford? Will it also be revenge against Gabrielle Hart – against me?"

She shut down the computer and hurried from the library. She still had a few minutes before her mum would be there, so she headed back to the assembly hall to pick up her things, trying to digest what she had just learned.

The assembly hall was silent. Bree was alone.

Or so she thought.

She suddenly heard the soft scraping of feet, the sound of someone running down the aisle.

"Who's there?" she called out, stepping from backstage out onto the stage. She saw no one. "Hello?"

A shadow moved at the back of the theatre.

"Who is it?" Bree called again, staring intently into the darkness.

She saw a quick movement near the bottom of the stairs leading up to the balcony. Then a figure stepped into a small pool of light cast from above.

Bree caught a momentary glimpse of a face, half in light, half in shadow.

It was the face of a girl, a girl about her age, but Bree couldn't place her.

"What are you doing here?" Bree cried out.

The girl said nothing. She simply turned and hurried up the stairs leading to the balcony.

Bree chased after the girl, racing to the stairs. A mysterious stranger lurking in the shadows of the theatre? Mysterious, yet familiar – just like the voice in the phone calls. In light of all that had happened, Bree felt certain that this was the person behind everything.

She was going to get her answers, and she was going to get them now, tonight, so that when the curtain went up tomorrow night, all this craziness would be behind her.

She dashed up the stairs, taking them two at a time. As she ran, she heard soft, steady footsteps charging ahead on the flight of stairs above her. Up she went, to the top level of the theatre. As she rounded each turn on the staircase, Bree caught a brief glimpse of a foot, or a leg, or a flash of colour vanishing around the bend ahead.

Once she reaches the balcony, there's nowhere else to go, Bree thought as her feet pounded the stairs. *I've got her. And she will tell me who she is and what has been going on!*

Reaching the top level of the staircase, she stepped out onto the balcony. Short rows of seats angled down towards the stage far below. A low railing ran across the front of the balcony. There Bree spotted the girl she had been chasing. The girl peered over the railing, looking down at the empty stage.

"There's nowhere to go, you know," Bree said firmly. "You can't run any more. I know you're the one who's been messing with me, playing these tricks, trying to make me believe that I'm crazy or that I shouldn't be in this play or who knows what. Well, it ends here."

She rushed down the aisle, walked up to the girl, and grabbed her by the shoulders.

"Who *are* you?" she demanded, spinning the girl around. For the first time she got a good look at her face.

Bree released the girl's shoulders. Were her eyes playing tricks on her? How could this be? Bree stared right into the girl's eyes. The face belonged to . . . Bree! She was looking at her own face, staring at herself.

"I'm not dreaming, am I?" Bree asked.

The other girl, the other Bree, shook her head.

"Then what's happening to me?" Bree shouted, venting all her anger and frustration in one powerful outburst.

The other Bree spoke in a voice that Bree had come to know all too well.

"Leave now, and never come back . . . or you'll be sorry!"

Bree was so stunned by hearing those same words, spoken with that familiar voice – her own voice – that she stumbled backward towards the stairs. Trying to regain her balance, as her mind tried to make sense of what had just happened, she tripped at the top of the stairs.

She went tumbling down the staircase and hit her head on the landing.

That last thing she saw before everything went dark was her own face looking down at her from the top of the stairs. The other Bree was smiling.

CHAPTER 14

Bree opened her eyes slowly. At first she could not make sense of her surroundings. She felt her head resting on a pillow.

Her awareness then shifted from the softness of the pillow to the throbbing pain in her head. Her blurry vision began to clear, and she could make out a rectangular plastic light cover, the type used to cover fluorescent bulbs in office buildings and hospitals.

Bree next focused on the ring of faces looking down at her.

Mum? Dad? Megan? What's going on?

"Where am I?" she asked, finally mustering enough energy to speak.

"You're in the hospital, sweetheart," her mum replied.

"That was quite a fall you took, but the doctors say you're going to be fine."

"Nice to see you awake, kiddo," her dad added.

"You'll do anything for attention, won't you, little sister?" Megan asked, smiling a genuinely warm smile.

"Fall? I really did fall?" Bree asked, still very confused. "That wasn't a dream?"

"No, honey, I wish it had been just a dream," her mum said.

"What day is it?" Bree asked, trying to sit up, but only managing to lift her head a few centimetres before falling back down onto the pillow. "What about the play? What happened to the play? Did the show go on?"

"Relax, honey," her mum said, gently stroking Bree's forehead. "You've been here for two days. The play was supposed to open yesterday, but of course, the opening was postponed after your fall."

"You can't put on a play without the lead, after all," Megan said.

"And, of course, everyone was so relieved that the play was postponed," her mum continued.

"What do you mean, relieved?" Bree asked.

"Because of what happened," Megan said. She grabbed

a remote and flipped on the TV, which hung above Bree's hospital bed. Megan dialled around until she found a news report.

"Crews are still cleaning up the small explosion that took place yesterday evening in the assembly hall of Moorwood Secondary School," the news announcer reported. "The blast went off at seven-thirty, which was the precise time a play at the school was about to begin. Fortunately, the play had been postponed, and so the assembly hall was empty at the time of the blast. No one was injured. Clean-up crews have been working around the clock to get that section of the school open and safe for use again."

Megan turned off the TV.

"The blast happened exactly at the moment I would have gone onstage to begin the play!" Bree said, trying again to sit up and once again falling back onto her pillow.

"Don't get excited, honey," her mum said. "You were very lucky. I'm not happy you fell, but when I think about what might have happened if the play had gone on . . ."

"In my dream I saw myself out onstage," Bree began to rant. "And I watched from above as I was about to start the play. I saw that explosion happen before it happened!"

She paused. If it sounded strange to her, imagine how it must sound to her family.

"Get some rest, honey," her mother said. "You've been through a lot."

Bree closed her eyes and tried to make sense of everything. Could the other Bree she saw have placed that dream into her mind, the dream in which she saw what would have happened if she'd gone out to start the play? And when she didn't heed that warning, did her other self show up at the theatre, while Bree was awake, to warn her in person?

With these questions swirling through her mind, and her body still weak and tired from the fall, Bree drifted off into a deep sleep. She fell gently into a dream, but this time the dream was calming and beautiful rather than terrifying.

In her dream, she was walking through a field of flowers on a beautiful, sunny day. As she strolled through the field, Bree was joined by her other self. It felt like the most natural thing in the world. It felt like an old friend had decided to accompany Bree on her stroll.

"The play is cursed, you know," the other Bree explained as they walked. "Whether by explosion, or a light falling, or some other way, whoever plays the lead is destined to die."

"Somehow I did know that, or I sensed it or something," Bree said. "But who are you?"

"It's a little complicated," the other Bree replied. "I'm you. Or rather, I am your spirit. I'm the ghost of the Bree who would have played the lead and died in the explosion if she hadn't tripped and fallen."

"So you died?" Bree asked. "I mean, I died?"

"Sort of," the other Bree said. "There are many timelines that run parallel to one another. They are based on the choices we each make a hundred times a day. Things like, 'Do I walk or take the bus?' 'Do I go to my friend's house or hang out at home?' 'Do I go to see the seven o'clock showing of a film or the eight o'clock one?' Simple choices like that.

"Every so often two of the timelines intersect. In our case, I made them intersect. With your help. Each of the dreams you had in which you saw me opened a portal between timelines. That portal allowed me to pass back and forth between timelines.

"By the time you had that last dream, the portal was stable enough that I was able to come through and stay in your timeline. That was how I was able to visit you in the theatre. I know this is all quite confusing."

"No, I think I understand," Bree said. "You are from the timeline in which I chose to go out onstage on opening night and do the play. And in that timeline, I died. You are my spirit from that timeline. You crossed over to my timeline, hoping to stop me from going onstage on opening night.

"I watched as the explosion happened and I was buried in rubble. I saw what was supposed to happen, in my dream, but it was because of my other self – because of you – that the show did not go on and I didn't get caught in the explosion.

"It was you! You were trying to warn me all along. You were trying to keep me from walking out onto that stage, either by scaring me out of the play or by calling me and telling me to leave. All that, all these weird things that have been happening to me, was just *me* trying to warn *me*."

"Exactly," the other Bree said. "I tried to prevent you from being on that stage when the explosion happened. And because of the way the timelines worked, I could only really do things that were part of the play. That's why it seemed like the scary things in the play were coming true in your real life. It was all I had to work with.

"I succeeded in getting you away from the stage on opening night, though your falling was never part of my plan. I also did it for selfish reasons. I did it to free myself and finally allow my spirit to rest."

"I don't understand," Bree said.

"It's part of the curse of the play," the spirit explained. "Not only does the girl playing the lead die, but she is cursed to be stuck inside the play, reliving it day after day, doing all the scary things that happen again and again, just like the girl who died thirty years ago, the first girl to ever play the role."

"That's why I was able to watch *her* performance in one of my dreams!" Bree suddenly realised. "She is stuck in the play, doing it over and over, dying again and again. One of those times I was able to watch her through my dreams. Just like I saw you die in my dreams."

"That's when I crossed timelines and was able to enter your physical reality in the theatre that night," the other Bree said. "But I couldn't work out how to warn you in any way you would actually believe me.

"And now that you are safe, I am finally free to rest in peace."

Before Bree could say anything else, her other self smiled and faded away, leaving Bree standing in the field of flowers with an overwhelming feeling of peace. Just before her dream faded, leaving her in the deepest, most restful sleep she had experienced in weeks, Bree thought about the good things that being in the play had done for her. She thought about how being involved with the play had given her the confidence to go onstage again and break out of her shell. Only next time, she would do it in a play that was not cursed!

After a few more days in the hospital, Bree finally went home. She rested at home for another week before she felt well enough to return to school. On her first day back, before classes, a meeting of the cast of *The Last Sleepover* was called to decide the fate of the play. With the assembly hall still under reconstruction, the meeting was held in the gym hall.

Being back in school for the first time since her accident, Bree felt surprisingly calm. All the fears, doubts and anxieties that had plagued her for weeks had vanished along with her spirit self when her dream had ended.

Stepping into the gym hall, Bree was greeted by a standing ovation.

"Welcome back, Bree!" Melissa shrieked, rushing over to Bree and throwing her arms around her. "This school is just not the same without you!"

"It's great to be back," Bree said.

"All right, everyone, please take a seat," boomed someone from the front of the gym.

Bree turned her head, along with everyone else. She knew from the voice that the speaker was not Ms Hollows, but rather a tall man walking with a cane.

"Hello, everyone. For those of you who don't know me, I'm Mr Gomez," he began. "I'm the Drama teacher here at Moorwood. I was also supposed to have been your director for this year's play, but unfortunately, I broke my leg shortly before rehearsals were to begin."

"What happened to Ms Hollows?" Melissa asked.

"She was only hired to direct that one play," Mr Gomez explained. "And since the performance got postponed, and I was able to return to work, she has left the school."

"I won't miss her," Tiffany whispered, leaning close to Bree's ear. "She was weird."

Wow, even Tiffany's being nice to me, Bree thought, smiling.

"And so now we come to the question of the fate of the play," Mr Gomez continued. Beside him, on a chair, sat a pile of copies of *The Last Sleepover*. "As you know, all future productions will be put on here in the gym hall until the repair of the assembly hall is complete. Since you have worked so hard rehearsing *The Last Sleepover*, I thought maybe we could talk about restaging it here. What does everyone think?"

Before anyone could speak, Mr Jenkins, the school caretaker, walked in.

"Sorry for the interruption, folks," he said, then went about lifting a large plastic bag full of garbage from the gym hall's rubbish bin.

Without saying a word, Bree stood up and walked over to the stack of scripts.

"We may do a play in the gym, Mr Gomez, but it won't be this play," she said, gathering up the pile of scripts in her arms.

"Wait a minute, please, Mr Jenkins!" she called out, walking across the gleaming wooden gym hall floor.

Reaching the caretaker, she pulled open the large plastic bag of rubbish, then turned back towards Mr Gomez.

"In fact, Mr Gomez, no one will ever perform this play again."

Bree dumped every copy of *The Last Sleepover* into the rubbish bag before returning to her seat. "Now," she began. "Which play would we all like to do instead?"

EPILOGUE
THIRTY YEARS LATER...

Bree slowed her car as she approached the school. She always enjoyed driving up to Moorwood Secondary School. It brought back a flood of good memories about close friends and fun times.

Today Bree was here to pick up her daughter, Elle, following Elle's Drama rehearsal. Bree was so pleased that Elle – short for Gabrielle – had shown an interest in theatre, recalling how much her own involvement with school plays when she was younger had added to her enjoyment of being a pupil here.

As Bree sat in the car with the window down, she noticed an odd-looking woman standing near the entrance to the school. The woman was tall and had medium-length, jet-black hair. She wore a long, dark coat.

Who is that woman? she thought. The woman turned around, revealing dark circles around her eyes.

"Ms Hollows!" Bree gasped.

She paused for a moment and caught herself. This woman looked younger than Bree herself. "There's no way that could be Ms Hollows," she said to herself. "That was thirty years ago, and Ms Hollows would have to be in her sixties by now."

Still, Bree was surprised, as she watched the woman disappear into the school building, by just how deeply the idea of seeing Ms Hollows affected her after all these years.

A few minutes later Elle came bounding out of the school. She ran up to Bree's car, bursting with excitement.

"Hey, Peanut, how was Drama rehearsal?" she asked as Elle slipped into the seat beside her.

"Fantastic, Mum," Elle replied. "You're not going to believe this. My Drama teacher found an old play in a trunk in the basement of the school. She told us that no one has put on the play in years!"

"Really?" Bree asked, starting the car. "What's the name of the play?"

"It's called *The Last Sleepover*," Elle explained. "And I'm just dying to play the lead!"

DO NOT FEAR—
WE HAVE ANOTHER CREEPY TALE FOR YOU!

TURN THE PAGE FOR A SNEAK PEEK AT

You're invited to a

CREEPOVER™

Truth or Dare

Abby Miller stared at the contents of the supermarket trolley. "OK, we've got peanuts, we've got veggies and dip, we've got popcorn," she said. "Do we need anything else?"

"What about crisps?" Leah Rosen, Abby's best friend, asked.

Abby nodded. "You go and get some crisps and I'll find something good to drink."

Leah disappeared around the corner, leaving the trolley behind for Abby. Abby wandered through the shop to the fridge section and stood in front of the juices, weighing up the options: apple or orange or tropical or—

Suddenly Abby had the creepiest feeling that she was being watched. In the chrome edges of the fridge, she thought she saw something move.

But when she glanced behind her, no one was there. She was the only person in the aisle.

Abby turned back to the fridge and quickly made up her mind. She was reaching for a the apple juice when—

"BOO!"

Abby shrieked as she felt a swift tug on her hair. She spun around to see Leah grinning at her.

"Gotcha!" Leah exclaimed. "Wow, I really spooked you, huh? You've got goosebumps!"

"Yeah, from the fridge." Abby laughed, gesturing to the chilly air.

"Sure, Ab. Whatever you say," Leah replied, her eyes twinkling. "Check out what I got!"

Abby wrinkled her nose. "Barbecue crisps? You know I don't like barbecue!"

"More for me," Leah said with a grin. "Don't worry, you're covered." She tossed a bag of tortilla chips into the trolley and placed a jar of salsa next to it.

Abby added two cartons of apple juice. "We'll order the pizzas after everybody else gets to my house, so I think that's about everything we need."

Leah frowned. "You're forgetting one essential – dessert!"

"What's wrong with me?" Abby said, laughing. "What should we get? Biscuits?"

"Brownies?" suggested Leah. The girls exchanged a glance.

"Both!" they said at the same time.

"Come on, desserts are this way," Leah said as she pushed the trolley around the corner. Suddenly she backed up – right into Abby!

"Leah! What are you—" Abby began.

But Leah frantically waved her hands at her friend and whispered, "Shh! Shh!"

"What? What is it?" Abby asked as she followed Leah to the opposite end of the aisle.

Leah leaned close to Abby's ear and whispered, "Max! Max Menendez! He's right over there getting chocolate! Do I look OK?"

Abby reached out and smoothed out the bumps in her friend's blonde ponytail. It was no secret that Leah had a major crush on Max. Every time she was around him, she got so nervous that she could barely speak. "You look great," Abby assured Leah. "Want to go and say hi?"

"Are you crazy?" Leah gasped as she tried to get a

glimpse of her reflection in a freezer case's shiny silver handle.

"Come on!" Abby urged her friend as she gave Leah a little push. "This is a perfect opportunity to talk to him! I'll come with you."

But Leah shook her head. "I'll probably say something stupid," she replied. "Let's just wait here until he leaves."

"Come on, Leah!" Abby whispered. "How will you two ever go out if you won't talk to him? And this'll be a great story to tell Chloe and Nora at the party tonight."

"Party? What party?" a voice asked.

Leah and Abby spun around.

It was Max!

He smiled at the girls. "You're having a party and you didn't invite me?"

Abby looked at Leah, thinking it would be the perfect time for her friend to say *something* to Max. But Leah just stood there – as frozen as the peas across the aisle. Her eyes were so wide that she even looked a little scared.

"Um ... of course we didn't invite you," Abby said, grinning playfully as she tried to save the situation. "It's a sleepover party. No boys allowed."

"Well, *fine*," Max said, pretending to be hurt. "I'm busy, anyway."

"Oh yeah?" asked Abby. "Doing what?"

"Wouldn't you like to know?" Max said with a laugh. "Nah, I'm just joking. I'm going to see a film with Jake and Toby. I thought I'd grab some sweets and stuff beforehand."

"That's cool," Abby said as her eyes lit up. She didn't notice the way Leah began to watch her. "What are you guys going to see?"

"Don't know yet," Max replied. He laughed. "I mean, obviously some snacks were the priority, you know?"

"Well, have fun," Abby said. "We've got to go. See you later, Max."

"See you, guys," Max said. "Hey, Leah – heads up!"

Leah jumped as Max tossed a chocolate bar to her. "I've got too much," he said with a smile. "You want one?"

"Uh, yeah, sure," Leah stammered. "Th-thanks, Max."

Max flashed another grin at the girls as he sauntered down the aisle. As soon as he was gone, Leah grabbed Abby's arm. "Wow! *He* gave *me* a chocolate bar!"

Abby smiled at Leah's excitement. "Kind of," she pointed out. "You still have to pay for it."

But Leah was too distracted to pay attention to Abby. "Max is so cute!" she gushed. "I wish I didn't get so tongue-tied around him."

"Just relax," Abby said to her friend. "He's only a boy."

"Only a boy!" exclaimed Leah. "How are you not as in love with him as I am?"

Abby thought for a moment about Max's spiky black hair and his big smile. He was definitely a hottie – but there was a guy at school who Abby thought was even hotter. "Yeah, he's pretty great," she said carefully.

But Leah gave Abby a piercing look. "You think there's somebody cuter than Max?" she asked. "Who?"

Abby pressed her lips together and shook her head. Her crush was top secret – and she wanted to keep it that way.

"Oh, come on, Abby," Leah begged. "I told you a million years ago that I liked Max. You owe me!"

Abby laughed. "I'm not telling. It's not my fault you can't keep your own secrets."

"I'll work out who it is," Leah said. "It's not Toby, is it?"

"Not even close," Abby replied. "Now would you please stop? I'm not telling!"

Leah clapped her hands. "I know! I know! It's Jake, isn't it?"

Abby's mouth dropped open. "No! Why would you even think that?"

"*Jake?*" squealed Leah. "Seriously? You like *Jake?*"

"No way," Abby said firmly. "Please, can you forget it? I mean it, Leah."

Leah sighed. "Fine, be that way. But I *will* find out for sure who you like."

Abby was silent as she pushed the trolley towards the fruit and veg aisle to get some strawberries for breakfast. She knew that when Leah was determined to find something out, there was no stopping her.

And Abby also knew that even though Leah was her very best friend, she couldn't keep a secret. Leah might be shy around boys, but she wasn't shy when it came to gossip. Abby knew she meant well, but telling Leah something in confidence was as good as posting it online.

Before long, the whole world would know it too.

After Abby and Leah finished buying everything they needed for the sleepover, Abby's mum drove them to

Abby's house. They had just started unloading the shopping when there was a loud knock at the door. Chester, the Millers' light-brown cocker spaniel, jumped up and ran towards the door, yipping in excitement.

"Woo-hoo!" Abby exclaimed as she hurried out of the kitchen. She flung open the front door to find her friend Nora Lewis waiting there, holding a purple rucksack, a pink sleeping bag and a stack of DVDs.

"Am I too early?" Nora asked as she walked inside. "My brother had to drop me off before he went to work."

"No, you're fine," said Abby. "Leah and I were just getting some snacks ready."

"Hey, Nora," Leah said, pouring the tortilla chips into a bowl. "Which films did you bring?"

Nora's brown eyes lit up. "I raided my brother's DVD stash!" she said excitedly as she spread three DVD cases across the worktop. "What do you think?"

Abby grabbed one of the cases and read the title. "*Attack of the Bee People?*" she asked.

"Oh, it's *sooo* funny," Nora said. "It's this film from for ever ago, and it was supposed to be really scary, but the special effects are horrible! It's hilarious!"

"What's this one?" asked Leah curiously. "*A Love Beyond*? Seriously?"

Nora sighed. "*Very* romantic. This guy dies, but he never stops loving this girl, even though she tries to go on with her life. My brother would kill me if it got out that he owned this."

Abby picked up the last DVD case, which had a black cover with a pair of spooky green eyes on it. "*The Hole*," she said as she read the title aloud. "This one looks scary."

"It is," Nora said, nodding. "It's about a cursed grave that can never be closed, and whenever anybody visits the person who was buried there, they get sucked into it too."

"Cool!" Leah exclaimed. "I love scary movies! Let's save that one for right before we go to sleep."

Abby shook her head as she dropped the DVD back on the worktop. "No way," she said firmly. "If we watch that one last, I'll be way too scared to sleep."

Leah laughed. "Exactly! Then we'll stay up all night for sure!"

There was another knock at the door.

"I'll get it," Abby said as she darted into the hallway. When she opened the front door, she found her friend

Chloe Chang waiting on the front porch. Chester barked in greeting.

"Hi, Abby!" said Chloe as she stepped inside. "Hi, Chester."

"I'm so glad you're here!" Abby exclaimed. "Leah and Nora are in the kitchen."

"Excellent," Chloe said as she gave Chester a pat on the head and followed Abby into the house. "I've been looking forward to this sleepover all day!"

"Hey!" Leah said as she waved to Chloe. "Abby, did you unpack the biscuits and brownies? I can't find them."

Abby shook her head. "Maybe we left a bag in the car," she replied. "I'll go and check." She grabbed her mum's car keys and hurried outside.

Abby's brown hair fluttered in the cool, damp breeze; in the distance, dark clouds threatened to bring a rainstorm before morning. She unlocked the car and found one last shopping bag that had fallen under the backseat.

Then Abby felt it again: that spooky sense that someone was watching her, just as she'd felt in the supermarket.

In the silence, she heard a crackling sound, like the crunch of fallen leaves. Almost like footsteps.

But that's not possible, she thought. Abby's house was

located at the end of a quiet street, next to a woodland nature reserve where people were forbidden to trespass. In all the years she'd lived there, Abby had never seen anyone in the woods.

She'd never stepped foot in them either, not with all the large NO TRESPASSING signs: bright-orange warnings that were impossible to miss.

But as she stood in the driveway, Abby couldn't shake the feeling that someone was standing just beyond the trees, watching her.

Then she heard another sound coming from the woods. This one was familiar, but she couldn't place it. It was sort of like the rusty squeak of an old swing on a stormy day, when the wind pushes the swing like invisible hands.

But there weren't any swings here.

Abby took a deep breath and spun around. "Hello?" she called loudly. "Who's there?"

The noise suddenly stopped. The silence was overwhelming.

Someone heard me, she thought.

"Hello?" she called again. A few moments passed. As she glanced at the nature reserve, Abby started to feel silly. *Are you some kind of baby?* she scolded herself. *Why are you getting all freaked out for absolutely no reason?*

Suddenly a creature burst out of the trees. The black blur took to the sky, cawing noisily, beating its wings with tremendous power as it flew away from the forest as fast as it could.

A crow, Abby thought with relief; she almost laughed out loud. *It was just a crow.* She grabbed the shopping bag and slammed the car door shut. She turned towards the house. She was eager to get inside and forget about the fear that had spread through her whole body as she stood, all alone, by the car.

The first thing Abby saw when she opened her door was Chester standing by the front window, growling quietly. She wanted to believe he was growling at the squirrels in the garden, but she couldn't help but think that the same thing that had spooked her had also spooked her dog. No matter how hard she tried, Abby couldn't stop thinking about the strange squeaking sound coming from somewhere in the woods, just beyond the trees.

And she couldn't shake the feeling that someone – or something – had been watching her.

WANT MORE CREEPINESS?

Then you're in luck, because P. J. Night has some more scares for you and your friends!

A TRUE TRANSFORMATION

Watch the creepy Drama teacher transform before your eyes!

1. Write MILDRED P WORMHOUSE on the blank.

_____

2. Delete all vowels except O and U.

_____

3. Move the eighth and ninth letters to the end.

_____

4. U equals LL. Replace.

_____

5. Delete all Ds, Ps and Rs.

_____

6. Insert an S between the first two consonants.

_____

7. Delete the third and fifth letters.

_____

8. Move the third letter to the last position.

_____

9. Move the seventh letter to the last position.

_____

YOU'RE INVITED TO ...
CREATE YOUR OWN SCARY STORY!

Do you want to turn your sleepover into a creepover? Writing and putting on a haunted play is a great way to set the mood. P. J. Night has written a few lines of dialogue to get you started. Fill in the rest of the scene and have fun scaring your friends.

You can also collaborate with your friends on this play by taking turns. Ask everyone at your sleepover to sit in a circle. Pick one person to start. She will fill in the first blank line of dialogue and then pass it to the next person. That person will fill in the next line of dialogue and pass it along. Once everyone has taken a turn, act out the scary play. Feel free to add as many parts as you have guests at your sleepover.

PERSON 1: I think I can hear something coming from the attic. It sounds like someone is crying ... or howling.

PERSON 2: It's probably just the wind, right?

PERSON 3: Perhaps, but haven't you heard the rumours? About ghosts appearing in attics late at night?

PERSON 1: Yes, but I don't believe in them. Who's brave enough to check out the attic with me?

_____

_____

_____

_____

_____

_____

_____

_____

_____

_____

_____

_____

_____

THE END

A lifelong night owl, **P. J. NIGHT** often works furiously into the wee hours of the morning, writing down spooky tales and dreaming up new stories of the supernatural and otherworldly. Although P. J.'s whereabouts are unknown at this time, we suspect the author lives in a drafty, old mansion where the floorboards creak when no one is there and the flickering candlelight creates shadows that creep along the walls. We truly wish we could tell you more, but we've been sworn to keep P. J.'s identity a secret ... and it's a secret we will take to our graves!